Whiskey Burn

Men of Cardosa Ranch

A Dark Romance

Gracin Saywer

Other books by Gracin Sawyer

Men of Cardosa Ranch
Branding Lily – Jacob and Lily's story
I'll Be What She Wants - Diesel and Samantha's story
Take Me Back - Carter and Callie's story
Whiskey Burn - Jax and Bryer's story
Burnt Skies - Bear and Hailey's story
Falling for London - Fox and Cadence's story

Copyright ©2023, 2025 Gracin Sawyer
Whiskey Burn
First Edition

ISBN: 9798313590844

All rights reserved.
No part of this book may be reproduced or transmitted in any form or by any means, electronic or mechanical, including photocopying, recording, or by any information storage and retrieval system without the written permission of the author, except for the use of brief quotations in a review.
This book is a work of fiction. Names, characters, places, and incidents are either products of the author's imagination or are used fictitiously. Any resemblance to actual persons, living or dead, events, or locales is entirely coincidental.

AUTHOR'S NOTE:

The reality that adults and children are taken every day and sold is an unfortunate truth. The threat is real. It is that very thing Jacob Cardosa has vowed to fight. His name, his riches, his power and sway... it all goes to saving them. He and his men, Diesel, Carter, Jax, Bear, and Fox, put their lives on the line to protect those they love. These books are their stories. Each told in an alternating POV and are complete with a happily ever after ending, while holding an overall series arc. Each book has a different level of darkness and sexual intensity. Thank you for reading.

A Warning from Jax Harper

Some men hurt. Some men heal.

I've been both.

This story? It's not gentle. It's not safe. It's survival. It's trauma. It's what happens when the past won't let go. If you're still reading, then you've been warned.

✓ Domestic Abuse & Manipulation – Bryer grew up in it. She lived in it. She stayed when she shouldn't have because fear is a hell of a leash.

✓ Child Abuse & Implied CSA – No child should go through what she did. But her mother? She used her like currency.

✓ Severe Trust Issues & Trauma Responses – She doesn't trust men. Can't. Won't. Not after what's been done to her.

✓ Possessiveness & Obsession – I'm older. I should be patient. But with her? I don't fucking share.

✓ Primal Chase Scene – Fear kept her caged her whole damn life. I showed her it could set her free.

✓ Toothpick Scene (Taste & Control) – She's mine. And when I want a taste of what's mine? I take it.

✓ Kidnapping & Series Arc Expansion – Bandito took her. He thought she was weak. He was wrong.

✓ Explicit Sexual Content & Age Gap Romance – I play. I tease. I push. And she learns that trust? It doesn't have to hurt.

She's my beauty—bruised, but never broken. And me? I'm the beast who'd burn the whole damn world to keep her safe.

She survived her past. Now she gets to live. With me.

If you're still here, you know what you're getting into. This ain't a love story for the faint of heart.

For the ones who learned fear before they learned love.

For the ones who stayed when they should have run—because leaving wasn't as simple as everyone thought.

For the ones who carry the past in their bones, who flinch at shadows, who know what it means to survive when survival never felt like a choice.

This wasn't easy to write. **It won't be easy to read.** But if you've ever felt like Bryer, like I have—**know this:**

You are more than what was done to you. **You are still here.**

And that means you win. Every damn time.

Chapter 1

Bryer

(7 years ago)

"You're nothing more than a slut."

Little did he know, I only had sex once. And it fucking sucked.

The man's words struck my soul. The last one stung, breaking into my heart like a thief, threatening to take the last bit of hope I had hidden.

I pushed against his chest and turned my head. *How did I get here?* The room spun around me as I tried to breathe.

Screaming for help wouldn't do any good. No one would hear me or come running to my rescue. There was no such thing as a knight in shining armor.

"You spread your legs for that boy. You can do it for me." His breath smelled like beer. He pressed his body weight on me with a strength I couldn't compete with. His hands gripped my wrists as I struggled to get away.

Tears felt like acid on my cheeks. Little good they did me.

Saying no wasn't an option. I would get in trouble with my mom. It was probably her who invited him over.

A small whimper escaped, "Please, stop."

His attempt at a kiss turned my stomach. The gross, slobbery saliva filled my mouth. "Shh, just take it."

His free hand pushed at my pants.

I prayed to God, but I didn't think he heard me. I was forgotten and probably disgusted Him too. He wouldn't listen to my prayers. But it didn't stop me from pleading for some kind of divine intervention.

The man slowed his movements, and just as his hand grazed my bare thigh, inching toward my center, his half-laden eyelids drooped even more. He slumped over me, his body crushing mine.

I didn't care about suffocating. He had passed out, and I had a way to escape. I pushed his shoulders. *Why was he so heavy?* I struggled to crawl out from under him. Thankfully, inch by inch, I found freedom.

Wrapping my arms around my stomach, I ran to my room and fought to control the tears and the urge to throw up.

Slut.
Whore.
You'd do anything for a guy.
Disappointment.
You can't say no.
Do that... Touch this... Kiss here.

Most fifteen-year-olds got praise from their parents for an A in school. But my mother was a bit... *malicious.* Praise came when she could tear me down after doing everything she instructed. Usually, her teachings were how to give the perfect blow job or how to let my body be used as someone saw fit. It came in the form of a male who wanted pleasure. How I'd escaped rape was beyond me. But tonight was close. Too close.

Wiping the tears from my face, I snuck out of my room and out the back door. The sky was dark, with a million stars watching me. I could almost hear their disapproval of me too.

I usually blocked everything out, separating myself from my body. I was good at that. I'd imagine a man who didn't exist coming to save me. He would protect me and take me far away.

If I could roll my eyes at myself, I would have. There was no such thing. I needed to let go of that single sliver of hope that not all men were evil.

"Hey." His voice scared me, but I recognized my best friend's silhouette as he joined me on the back steps of the old trailer house I lived in with my mother and her third husband, Rick. Dani lived across the street and was as close to any guardian angel as I'd ever get. But not even he could save me.

In my eyes, he wasn't a boy or a man... he was just Dani. At school, he was the heartthrob of the football team, but here at home, he was my rock.

He must have seen the light on in my room because the rest of the house was dark and empty, aside from the unconscious guy on the living room floor.

Rick and my mom were gone again. I didn't even know when to expect them home. It could be hours or days. I never knew.

I sucked in a shaky breath. "Hey."

He looked me over, and a glare turned his gaze cold. "You okay?"

I nodded as he pulled me in, wrapping his arm around my shoulder. He was the only boy I trusted. We'd even experimented one night and tried to kiss, but it was like kissing a brother. We both cringed and began laughing. Nope. We were nothing more than friends.

He was tense. "I will kill him."

I shook my head, instantly panicked. Dani wasn't scared of fighting. I'd seen it firsthand when he beat up his best friend for taking my virginity. I'd also seen him in handcuffs for other fights. He wasn't afraid of anything. "You can't go back to juvie." The coach would kick him off the team if he had one more infraction. Living in a small town was his only saving grace. There weren't enough boys to make a team without him.

But if he killed someone, he might never come out of jail. Maybe they'd send him to prison at eighteen. That was worse than anything the coach could do to him.

He kissed the top of my head. "It ain't right."

Tears threatened to spill as we sat there, staring at the sky.

"I deserve it," I said before I could stop myself.

"Fuck that, Bry. You deserve the world. If they can't promise you the sky and all the stars, you just keep running." A shooting star raced over us, and I remembered how he told me he'd run with me. But I couldn't do that to him. To his dad.

At fifteen, we both had seen more than our fair share of pain. His mother killed herself. He found her in their house. I wondered what it would be like to find my mother that way.

"Promise me." His voice was low. I lifted my head to see his dark features as he stared at me. "Promise me you'll get as far from here as you can. Promise me you'll live. You are worth so much more than this."

I nodded, unable to speak. I couldn't promise him anything.

The front door slammed shut, and I jumped. Fight or flight took over, and I was ready to bolt. The drunk man stumbled out and headed to a car. He mumbled something about a bitch and got in the driver's seat. I hoped he would drive his car off a cliff.

Chapter 2

Jax
(Present Day)

"You may kiss the bride."

Cheers erupted throughout the small venue. Standing up with Jacob while he married Lily was an honor. My brothers all looked at each other with shit-eating grins when he deepened the kiss enough to make the preacher blush.

Diesel, Flapjack, and I stood beside Jacob. While Sam, Callie, and Lily's childhood friend, Emily, flanked Lily.

Sam gave Diesel a smile that spoke volumes of how their night would be going. But damn if it didn't compete with Callie and Flapjack's flirting. They were all a hot mess. It was a good thing they were getting their own places soon. The walls were thin in the bunkhouse, and there was not enough wide-open space in Nevada to drown out the noise.

Jacob decided it was time to start building a few more homes on the ranch. There ain't no way he would separate us, but it was clear we needed more room... to grow.

I wasn't complaining.

Hell, maybe one day I'd have someone to bring to the ranch and make a little noise of our own. I didn't like quiet, casual sex. You weren't doing it right if you couldn't make her scream.

I didn't think Flapjack would take my advice so seriously with me in the next room.

I wasn't into public voyeurism. And hearing them through the walls was cutting painfully close. Fuck, I might as well be in the same room watching. However... private *observation* was entirely different.

Jacob led Lily down the aisle. Everyone stood, cheering as they passed.

Married.

That makes two of us who have officially tied the knot. However, Flapjack and Callie didn't wait for the wheels to touch the ground in Vegas before finding a chapel. I couldn't blame them. We'd just been through hell knowing Flapjack had been taken by a trafficking ring, and we went to save his ass.

The same asshole who kidnapped Callie took him to Panama. On the private island just off the city, they used girls of all ages for their insatiable pleasures. It made my skin crawl.

But those girls were safe now.

It was one of my jobs working for Jacob to check in on them once we were back in the States. Hundreds of girls we'd saved and placed in safe homes. And every single one I knew by name. They were more than a notch on a bedpost. More than just a face on a missing poster. More than whatever their bodies were used for. And I sure as hell wouldn't forget them.

My mind tried to wander down a different path. A darker memory of before...

I quickly shut it down and focused on the present. I wasn't on a mission. I was no longer in the SEALs. And I was no longer Jack Granger.

Jacob made sure to wipe my past clean, pulling strings no man on earth should have, and gave me a fresh start. Starting with my name. Jax Harper. Jack died eleven years ago.

With Jacob and Lily down the aisle, they were crowded by their guests, congratulating them. Doc, Lily's grandfather, wiped a tear from his cheek. He never got to walk his daughter down the aisle, but he was able to be here for Lily. He no longer lived at the ranch, living out his old age near the lake, fishing. But it was good to see him here tonight. He was family.

Maria cried while her husband, Lupe, sucked in a tear and coughed, trying to pretend he wasn't just as emotional. They were here living on a visa until Jacob could help them gain citizenship. After the fuckwad Dominic invaded their house trying to kidnap Sam, and Maria was shot, Jacob refused to leave them in Mexico. They were also family and needed to be here with us.

We've all had people ripped from our lives, driving us to be here. There wasn't one of us who hadn't lost someone. I think those who died before us were still here, their memories keeping us company. I know I won't forget. I couldn't.

A hand clamped down on my shoulder. "How does it feel to be the oldest single man here?"

Bear laughed and stepped with me to the reception area. I grimaced. Forty was only a month away.

Shit.

I wasn't *that* much older than my brothers. Diesel and Jacob were thirty. But Flapjack, Bear, and Fox were still in their twenties.

Double shit.

"Brother, I'm only old in age. I'll still kick your ass." I laughed and tapped the bar where open drinks were served. Ordering a whiskey sour, I sipped the beverage and leaned with an elbow on the counter. "I can't believe Jacob's married."

"Well, I think he was a goner as soon as you found Lily. She's had him wrapped around her finger ever since."

I remembered that night vividly. I was the one who found her and watched as she tried to take her own life. I still felt her blood under my fingers like a bad nightmare. She had been so scared and thought we were there to hurt her. Fuck… if she only knew then what she knows now. I watched her laugh at something Jacob said. "I think she has us all wrapped around her fingers."

It had been so long since I had a sister; bringing Lily into the family made me realize how much I was missing. There wasn't a damn thing I wouldn't do for her. I glanced at each '*brother*'. I'd protect my family with my own life.

Bear thumped me on the back. "You ain't kidding." Shaking his head, he ordered a beer. "You ever think about settling down?"

"I'm impressed you can even speak those words. I remember the first time we went on a hunt together. You puked afterward and swore you'd never have a girlfriend because—"

"Hey," Bear coughed. "I didn't puke."

"You did too! If you'd been a girl, I'd have been the one holding your hair back. You got it on my shoes. Trust me," I said, taking another sip. "You puked."

"Fucker." He chuckled and took a drink.

Laughing felt good. Even in the darkest of times, my brothers would find a way to get a laugh in. Without it, we'd all be consumed by the darkness and horrors in our lives. It was the only way to stay sane after seeing what we'd seen.

This family was tighter than any blood could create. Without them, I wouldn't be able to do this job. I wasn't sure I'd still be here. They helped me find a purpose... a place in this world where I can help.

We might save women and children, but it didn't mean we were good guys. We all have done bad things. And we'd continue to do them. Fuck the world and its rules.

I took another sip, lost in thought. The last mission still clung to me like a shadow. Everywhere I went, I saw the girls. I couldn't shake them, nor did I want to. I didn't want to forget because if I did... then they were nothing more than a job. I couldn't detach my humanity from work, or I'd become callous. I could feel it snake around my heart, begging me to flip the switch and lose myself to the darkness. It would be all too easy to forget.

But I didn't deserve easy. Every judgment placed on me was merited. I could justify every action, but in the end, I was still exactly what *they* had made me.

A killer.

A mercenary.

A vigilante.

An elusive ghost.

Although my brothers could claim a few of those titles as well. It's a bond between us, knowing we weren't alone.

Watching Jacob, I was happy for him, but my heart twinged. He'd found his happiness, but it was rare for a man in our world to find a woman who could be strong enough to endure the reality of what we did.

I smirked as I gazed over the other women in our family. Yeah, it definitely took a tough lady to be with one of us. Not that I ever expected to find anyone. Hell, I was pushing forty and had no false fantasies about meeting someone who could love me.

Shit. I really just needed to get drunk and stop thinking.

Chapter 3

Bryer

"Are you fucking stupid? Did you hear what I said? Get your ass out there and keep them happy. I don't pay you to stand there." Rick took a drink from his flask, which I'm sure was filled with something hard, and glared at me over the fingerprinted steel.

He hardly paid me enough to survive, but I'd take his yelling and demeaning abuse. It was much better than the alternative.

My stomach flipped as I slipped past my stepfather. I tensed, bracing myself for his abuse, but I made it to the reception area before he caught me—this time.

Plastering a smile on my face, I grabbed a tray of drinks and made my way through the crowd. The venue was perfect. Outdoors, with big white tents, hanging lanterns, and Edison lights, a large bar stocked with a plethora of drinks, autumn-colored flowers everywhere... The late afternoon air was warm but not overly hot for September in Northern Nevada.

The bride looked so happy, and while I had never known that kind of joy, it was nice to see. Her long dark hair was down, hanging in curls, and she wore the most beautiful dress that looked like the sequins were sewn to her body. But... while the groom towered over her, he never overshadowed her. She lit up the room while he stood back and let her shine. It was the way he looked at her that stole my breath. Never in my life did I ever think love could be seen in just a look. That was for romance novels and movies. But goosebumps broke out over my arms as I stalled beside one of the tables. I couldn't tear my eyes from them.

For a moment, a spark of hope flickered to life in my chest until I heard Rick calling for me from behind the main tent, where only staff was allowed. *Ugh.* How this man ever landed a catering job like this was beyond me. But then again... he would never show the public how he truly was. It was all an act. Mr. Popularity on the outside, cruel, heartless, sadistic devil on the inside.

I didn't understand how my mother could stay with him. It's like she craved his attention more than anyone. And he held it over her like a puppet.

Not me. I wanted to get far, far away. And I would. One day. It's just not as easy as people think. I wasn't even sure I could make it on my own, something Rich was great at reminding me of.

At twenty-two, all I had was a crappy studio apartment over my mother's garage, an old beater car that barely made it across town without breaking down, and about twenty dollars in the bank. No, wait, I splurged and grabbed a chicken sandwich for dinner last night, so I have nine dollars in the bank.

I need this job. I need this job. I need this job.

Working for Rich and my mother wasn't ideal, but Rich told everyone how incapable I was, and even the local gas station was leery of hiring me.

I need this job.

I picked up another empty beer bottle and glass from a table and set it on my tray before slipping through the crowd, handing off full drinks to the celebrating guests.

"Bryer!" Rick's voice boomed over the music, but not loud enough to disturb the reception.

I tensed. What in the world did I do now to piss him off? Did I breathe wrong?

Turning, I bumped into something solid and was thrown off my feet, falling backward. My tray landed with a crash, but firm hands caught me, preventing me from hitting the ground. My breath caught in my throat. I didn't run into something... rather *someone* who was built like a freaking mountain.

Looking up, his deep chocolate brown eyes bore straight through to my soul. There was no malice or hate penetrating through his gaze. I could have been mistaken, but it almost looked like... concern? Maybe I *did* hit my head.

"Oh, no... I'm so sorry. I didn't mean to run into you." I apologized profusely and tried to stand up on my own, but he never removed his hand.

Normally, that would trigger me or send me into a panic. But it oddly did neither of those things. I was hyper-aware of his hand placement and heat radiating through my uniform, but I wasn't scared.

He took me by the elbow. "Let me help you."

Oh shit. His voice was like that perfect mixture of deep and raspy, hitting all the right nerves and making my heart race. Or was it his hand still pressed to my back that had my body reacting like an addict craving more?

Once on my feet and standing, albeit on shaky legs, he removed his hands but dipped his head to look at me. "You okay?"

Yes. No. Yes. I don't know! I quickly grabbed the serving tray I'd dropped and held it close to my chest. "Yes, thank you. I really am sorry for running into you. Are you hurt?"

He chuckled. "Me? No, angel, no offense, but I doubt a little thing like you could do much damage to a guy like me."

I could feel the heat rising into my cheeks, neck, forehead... oh, God, my whole body was turning red. "I should get back to work. Again, I'm sorry." I picked up the empty bottles that had fallen with the tray.

"You can run into me anytime." He downed the last of his drink and winked.

He freaking winked at me! If my heart beat any faster, it would explode. I would die at twenty-two years of age of a twitter-pated heart attack.

I reached for the empty glass in his hands, but he held it back. "I think I'll walk with you, put it away myself. I'd never forgive myself if I let another man catch you, should you fall again."

Shit. Shit. Shit.

I was not used to flirting. Heck, I wasn't sure if I knew how to do it properly. I wish Dani were here... he could walk me through the steps, tell me what to say, and help me not appear like an idiot. Well, that last part was a stretch. I'm not even sure he could help with that.

With no words coming, I ducked my head and walked toward the back of the tent, where the servers slipped through the tiny exit to grab more entrees. I stopped just before the opening, holding out my hand to prevent the man, who smelled like leather, whiskey, and an intoxicating cologne, from following.

"Sorry, I can't let you back there." I kept holding my hand out for the empty glass. "Event rules."

He leaned in close enough I could almost taste his drink of choice in the air between us. "Rules don't apply to me."

My heart skipped. "The event rules or rules in general?"

"In general." He slipped past me and ducked through the entrance to the back. Setting his glass in the correct water basin for the dishwashers, he spun around to watch me.

It was a little unnerving. What if I fell again? I'd just hope the ground would swallow me whole because there was no way I'd come back from that a second time.

Behind the man, Rick marched toward us, but the look on his face was anything but happy. Shit. I was sure I would take the man's *'rules don't apply to me'* with a hand across my face.

"Bryer, what is he doing back here? You know guests aren't allowed behind the tent." His glare cut into me with a promise of what would happen for allowing anyone to see the real behind-the-scenes of Rick's business. He turned and plastered on the best fake smile I'd seen a million times. He was a professional at acting and creating an image he wanted people to see.

My stomach turned. Whatever the stranger thought of me didn't matter now. He was about to hear some story that Rick would conjure to make me look incapable and stupid. My stepfather was good enough at lying; he should have gone into politics. But thank God he didn't. I couldn't even imagine what a messed-up world we'd live in if he was in some sort of office, running an entire community! I shuddered and folded my arms, keeping the empty tray close to my body.

"I'm so sorry, there must have been a misunderstanding with my employee. We keep this part closed off from guests to keep you from seeing all the disorganized chaos behind the scenes." Rick laughed for good measure. All part of his act. "We just want you to have a great time and not worry about anything else. Let's get you another drink, and I'll make sure she gets the empty glasses picked up, so you won't have to worry about doing dishes yourself." Rick clamped a hand down on the man's shoulder and attempted to urge him through the door.

The stranger looked down at Rick's hand and back up at him. The toothpick twirling over his tongue stilled as he clenched it between his teeth. "She's done her job. Quite well, I might add." The toothpick twirled once. His upper lip curved ever so slightly. "I'll get my own drink when I'm ready."

Oh no. My stomach twisted and rolled. If only I could slip past them both and reach a more open spot. A public place where everyone could see. Behind the tent flaps, I was trapped and had no witnesses. Well, none that would admit to seeing anything.

I moved, hoping to make it, but Rick gripped my arm, stopping me. His fingers wrapped around me where the stranger couldn't see, digging into my flesh. It was painful. A warning. "Wait just a minute, sweetheart." His voice dripped with nauseating sweetness. "This gentleman needs a drink. It is your job to help all guests. Maybe he'd like you to help him? I'm sure the empty bottles will be there for you after you make sure he gets *whatever* he wants."

"Remove your hand." The stranger didn't move, but I didn't breathe. His jaw clenched as he glared at Rick. The flirty man from earlier was gone. He was tense and looked like a rattlesnake ready to strike.

Rick let go of me and cocked his head. "Of course." He grinned for the stranger's sake, but I knew hiding under that seething smile, there was a scorch of anger that would be taken out on me later tonight.

Fuck my life. If I had been more careful, watched where I was going, and not bumped into the man... Too late now. I would just have to take whatever was coming.

I moved my arm, not daring to cover the red marks already showing.

Cowering away, I slipped behind the stranger. "Let's go get that drink," I said way too cheerfully, but I wanted to break the intense staring session between the men. If anything, I needed to de-escalate the situation as much as possible.

The stranger stood tall and poised, ready to jump on Rick. Not that I'd stop him. I mean... I'd probably get the repercussions, but watching someone put my stepfather in his place would be fun.

Turning, the man's stare softened on me. No anger or hatred hid behind his look. It was a scary contrast to the second before. How easily he controlled himself. I wasn't sure if I was impressed or threatened. The butterflies in my stomach fluttered back to life, and I settled on the former. I was more than impressed. I was infatuated. Attracted? I definitely had a slight crush forming.

But that was scary. I didn't crush on men. And definitely not one who looked old enough to be my father.

Only a few grey hairs laced with his dark strands under his cowboy hat. Maybe he was in his thirties. Forties at most? He looked hard and strong. His entire frame was built like he worked in the gym daily. It was a bit intimidating because I was the opposite. With a roll around my middle, and when I tipped down, anyone could see my double chin. But I had other issues to contend with. My image wasn't something I had energy for.

"Alright, angel, lead the way." He gestured to the exit and followed me through.

"Bryer. My name is Bryer," I offered, ducking my head to hide the red in my cheeks. He didn't ask for my name, and I suddenly felt too brave and forward by giving it to him.

"Bryer. That's a beautiful name. I'm Jax." He said it as if he wanted me to know his name. Smooth, confident, and so... *Ugh*, it was so hard to focus around this man!

Jax. Well, at least I had a name to put with the face I'd see in my dreams tonight.

He touched my shoulder, not rough, but enough to stop me. He shook his head slightly. "Don't hide your face."

God. If I got any redder, I'd be a tomato. If I tried talking, I'd only stumble on my words. Nodding, I averted my eyes, purposely avoiding him.

"Angel," his deep voice rattled me to my core.

What was this man made of to make me so instantly drawn to him? I closed my eyes and forced myself to take a steady breath. I feared he would see straight through me, to the deepest, darkest parts. The part of me I worked so hard to keep hidden from the world. And if he saw it, would I see the disgust reflected in his perfect stare? I don't think I could live with him seeing the real me. My heart began to beat erratically. Fear clamped around my throat.

He touched my chin, tilting my head so I had to look at him. As soon as I opened my eyes, I was pulled into his intense gaze. Like a magnet, I was held in place, staring at this man who should be the definition of sex appeal in the dictionary.

"Never look down. Your worth is not found on the ground." His words hit my heart like an arrow, piercing me all the way through.

It took everything I had to not stumble back as his touch shot a flame of heat through me. Moving away from him was more challenging than keeping an ice cube from melting in hell. "How about we get you that drink?"

Chapter 4

Jax

Bryer.
Her name settled into my soul like a blanket of comfort.
Fuck.

My initial attraction to her increased with every look, every smile, every sound that flowed off her lips. But she was young. Too young. There was no logical reason I should even entertain the thought of this woman and myself.

Not to mention my line of work.

It felt like a hopeless dream to bring anyone into my life. Lily and Sam were the exception for Jacob and Diesel. And Callie… she was born into a world just as harsh with her father, the head of a small family in Michigan in the organized crime department. Yet my heart flared with hope I hadn't felt in years, since before the world tried to kill it all.

And damn if I didn't already feel protective over her. When her boss touched her, it took everything inside of me to remain calm. If he touched her again, I'd rip his arm off. It was a promise.

I never broke her stare as I twirled the toothpick over my tongue and took the drink she got for me at the bar. Our fingers touched, and my cock jumped.

Yeah, this girl would be the only thing I dreamed about tonight. It will be her face I see when I take the world's coldest shower.

A blush crept up her neck and cheeks as she pulled her hand back. "If you need anything else…"

Her chest heaved as she pulled in a long, steadying breath, and I tried really hard not to notice how her uniform strained with her breasts. *Fuck.* This girl had all the right curves.

I wanted to grip her thighs and hold her to me as I suffocated between her legs.

I had never been so intensely attracted to a woman as I was right then. It was like the universe was teasing me with something else I could never have.

"Bry!" A younger man waved her down from the other side of the venue. He couldn't be much older than her, and I instantly felt jealous of their relationship. I wondered if it was her boyfriend. I hoped not. I didn't think I would be okay with another man touching her.

Shit. I needed to walk away before I killed someone.

She smiled and ducked her head before heading his way. I leaned against the bar and watched while taking my drink in one swig. His hand went to her waist as he leaned in, kissing her on the cheek. He had a genuine grin for her and said something that made her laugh. I had to set the glass down before it shattered under my grip. I wanted to be the reason for that smile, that laugh, that look.

I tapped the bar. "Can I get another drink? Make it a double and keep it neat." I couldn't pry my eyes away from Bryer and the man.

Imagining ways to end his life came like second nature. One method for each touch, each smile he pulled from her, each lingering gaze... one for every second he spent in her presence like he belonged there.

Bear filled the space next to me. He still had a beer in his hand as he leaned back against the bar. "I'm not sure I like that look, brother."

I downed my drink and tore my eyes from the beauty across the room. "What look?"

"Like you're gonna murder someone." He chuckled. "I've seen it enough to know." He turned to scan the room, landing on the man and my girl. "How many ways did you imagine killing him?"

"I don't know what you're talking about."

He laughed and tipped his bottle back, taking a drink. "Fuck you don't."

"Too many times," I grumbled. It wasn't hard for me to spot the man waiting outside the venue.

Bryer's sweet voice carried through the crowd and over the music. It would take a lifetime to remove that sound from my soul.

My stomach flipped. I wasn't one to become so attached to anyone so quickly. But as soon as she ran into me, it felt so real. It felt like... I was home. I was me. The real me.

I gave Bear the best '*fuck you*' grin and ordered another drink. He looked the most menacing of all of us '*brothers.*' Hell, he was like a brick covered in tattoos. But the kids we saved gravitated to him like candy. He might have been scary as hell, but his name fit him well.

He and I had grown close over the years. When Jacob recruited him, I was leery, but he became my closest brother. It made sense he knew me so well.

I watched the stranger, wanting him to do something to warrant me beating his ass. Nothing. Damn it. I didn't even get a bad vibe from him. I think that pissed me off more.

Fuck. It's not like I had any claim on Bryer. But damn... for the first time, I wanted to have more. There was something about her I wanted to protect. I wanted to wrap my arms around her and block her from the world. I wanted to kill anyone who got too close.

This entire thing was so confusing. I just met her. But as soon as her body collided with mine, it was like a missing piece of the puzzle fell into place. It was like intuition. When you meet someone and just know instantly, like her jerk of a boss. There was nothing about that man that was good. Discernment was a great gift, and right now, everything in my mind, heart, and body told me SHE was the one.

"We could make it look like an accident." Bear jarred me from my thoughts.

"What?"

He nodded subtly to the guy. "No solo missions."

"Shit. Bear, we can't kill him."

He shrugged. "Why not?"

I nearly choked trying to come up with a good excuse. But aside from his lingering gaze on Bryer, I had none. He watched her as if he was ready to jump in front of a bus for her. And it pissed me off.

I warred with my thoughts and heart. On the one hand, I was relieved she was protected, but on the other hand, I wanted to be the only man to offer her that protection.

"Is she worth it?" Bear's eyes followed Bryer to where she disappeared behind the tent's exit.

"Aren't they all?" All life had value, but I knew that wasn't what he asked. Yet, I couldn't bring myself to say out loud how I truly felt because... well, shit, I didn't know, aside from wanting to murder anyone who breathed in Bryer's direction.

I felt a heavy stare land on me. Loverboy stood with his arms crossed and a glare shooting through the space between us. I had to admit, it would have been intimidating if I had been any other man. He was doing his best, but it only made me laugh. He had no idea who the hell he was staring down. I nudged Bear with my elbow. "It might be time to have a chat."

Bear grinned over his beer. "A chat? I thought you said we can't kill him?"

"You know what I mean. Shut up and go dance with a pretty girl. Hell, steal Sam from Diesel if you're looking for a bit of fun." I heard him mumble something about a great idea as I strode toward the party crasher.

I twirled my toothpick over my tongue. It was a habit of sorts I picked up to keep my head clear and emotions calm. It gave me something to focus on and keep me in the moment.

"Friend of the bride or groom?" I asked, stopping at the edge of the tent. I knew he was neither. Every guest was vetted, and we knew exactly who was invited or allowed to be there.

Though apparently, we lacked in the catering department. If Jacob had met with Bryer's boss, there was no way he would have hired him. But then, I wouldn't have met *her*.

The man's stare flicked to Bryer, who I saw enter the tent from the corner of my eye. Already, I knew her body, her stride, her feeling. I could still smell her, so I had that too. It wouldn't be long, and I'd know the sound her steps made. I'd spend a lifetime learning all the small quips, like if a hitch in her breath meant she was excited or scared.

Instantly, I pictured her excited, her chest rising to catch her breath as I worked to hear the sound again. I wanted to elicit a moan and hear my name roll with it. I could almost hear the sound as I pictured her beneath me on a bed, her fists in the sheets as I…

FUCK.

Whoever said instant attraction or obsession or love wasn't real, lied. Because I was, without a doubt, obsessed. And now I had a hard-on and a need to do exactly what I imagined.

"Don't look at her." I was two seconds away from ripping the man's eyes out. "You look at me."

His glare snapped back to me. "You're the one eye-fucking her. She's not a one-night stand. Keep your hands and dick off her."

I almost laughed in his face. "You say that as if you could stop me."

He shifted slightly but remained tense. "Listen, I don't know who you are, Pops, but Bryer is not just some girl you can fuck. Trust me, just leave her alone."

Every intuition I've ever had was nothing compared to the warning I felt deep in my soul with his words. Something wasn't right. "Well, we can agree on one thing. She's not someone's fuck toy."

His glare turned into something more… curious. "So, you weren't imagining screwing my girl?"

His girl? Damn it.

Bryer's arm brushed mine, and a thousand electric sparks raced through me. Her smile lit up her eyes, but the tinge of a slight blush warmed her gaze. "I see you two have met." She turned to the guy. "I have to stay and do clean up. You might as well leave. I can call you after for a ride?"

He didn't stop staring at me. His teeth grinding as he contemplated leaving.

Turning to her, I ignored his annoyance. If she was in the room, only she deserved my attention. "I can take you wherever you need to go. I'll be here until everyone leaves. Part of *my* job."

"And what job is that?" He glowered, and it was almost amusing to watch him grasp for anything to use.

"Security."

I didn't miss how Bryer shifted with that word. Something much deeper was going on. And now I wasn't going to give up until I knew.

"I'll just wait in the car. I don't got anywhere else to be." He was really going to make me pull rank in a minute.

She offered a nervous chuckle. It didn't sit well with me. "Dani, you'll be sitting there for hours. I doubt I'll be done until after midnight."

He touched her elbow. "Is Rick here?"

"You know he is." Was that disappointment or something more in her voice?

Dani shook his head. "Then I'll stay."

Bryer flicked her gaze to me before looking at him. "Thanks." She looked over her shoulder. "I better get back to work."

She wove herself through the reception, smiling at everyone.

"There you go, eye-fucking her again."

I twirled the toothpick once and fought to keep my shit together before pummeling him into the ground. "If I were her boyfriend and I thought someone was *eye-fucking* her, they wouldn't survive the night with their eyes intact."

"Listen, old man, I'm not her boyfriend, but I sure as hell ain't about to let someone hurt her."

Wait. Bryer wasn't his girlfriend? Damn. My heart jumped, and my brain screamed that whatever cliff it was about to dive off was a bad idea, but I didn't listen.

I grinned. "It was nice to meet you, Dani."

Walking away, I could hear him cursing, but he left toward the parking lot while I found a seat to watch my beauty for the night.

Chapter 5

Bryer

My heart raced as I felt *his* eyes on me for the rest of the night. He watched me like I was the one he was protecting.

Security.

Of course he was. It made sense. He was intense and fierce, and I'm sure he could use those muscles to subdue any man here. I wondered if he trained to fight?

It was just after two in the morning, and I was dragging after cleaning up, but Jax was still there, watching. There was no way I was looking like anything less than a zombie at that moment, but he looked at me as if I were the most beautiful woman in town.

The bride and groom had long since left, as had all the guests except him and one other man who looked scary mean, but I didn't feel wary of him. Another oddity for me tonight.

Rick ordered the tents to come down and walked over to me. He searched the spacious area, and his eyes hardened when he spotted Jax. "What are they still doing here?"

I shrugged. "I don't know. I think they were the event security or something. I don't think they're leaving until we're all done." I hoped not. They were a buffer I needed, even if they didn't know it. With them there, Rick wasn't likely to do anything.

My stepfather ground his teeth briefly and then looked at his watch. "I expect you to show up for your shift tomorrow. I guess you better go ahead and get out of here while I clean up for you."

Clean up for me? There was nothing left to clean. I bit my tongue to stop myself from retorting something that would end in a painful bruise. Besides, I was too tired to argue. And, of course, I couldn't get anyone to change shifts for me tomorrow, and I had less than three hours to be back up and open the doors to Silversmith's at six. To be fair, plenty of servers were willing to trade, but Rick denied each one.

Silversmith's was a lucrative adventure for Rick and my mom, but the public didn't see the real owners. It was scary how sick and twisted people could hide among communities of any size.

As soon as I made my way toward the parking lot, Jax moved, walking right to me. His grin melted my insides. "I'll walk you. I promised I wouldn't let another man catch you. I meant it."

Even at two in the morning and dragging ass, he made a blush creep over my cheeks. Honestly, I'd been on fire the entire night with his eyes on me. I tucked a rogue strand of hair behind my ear and ducked to keep my eyes from trailing over him.

He touched my waist, heat searing through me from his fingertips. "Whoa, angel." He tipped my head up with his thumb. "I told you not to look down. I want to see that blush when you look at me."

God, what this man did to me! I think I forgot how to breathe.

He hooked his hand under my elbow. "Come on, angel. Let's get you out of here and home so you can sleep."

"Why are you still here?" I asked, trying to devise any excuse to make him talk more.

"I thought you knew." His body was now so close that my arm brushed his waist. "You."

"Me?"

He chuckled. "Security. Remember? I had to make sure you were safe."

"Like a personal bodyguard." I meant it to come out as a joke, but I failed. Miserably.

"Exactly." He nodded toward the only running car in the parking lot. "I assume that's for you? I'd be lying if I said I wasn't hoping he'd just go home so I could do the honors myself."

Was that creepy? Did he actually want to take me home or... No. Bryer, stop it. Being around him has made you feel safer than you've felt in years. He isn't going to kidnap you.

"Yeah, my car tire decided now was a good time to deflate." Another bad joke. But I wasn't lying. The stupid thing had a flat tire, and I had no spare, donut, or money to fix it. So, it would have to stay right where I left it, about a block away.

"I guess it's a good thing you have such a good *friend* to help you at two in the morning."

Was that him sounding jealous, or my imagination?

"Dani is like a brother. I can't imagine him not being here. He's always got my back." I wasn't sure why I was suddenly divulging so much, but I couldn't stop myself from wanting to make sure he knew Dani and I weren't a couple.

The late fall night air was chilly, and I shivered. Wrapping my arms around my middle, I tried to conserve my body heat because I didn't want to rush to Dani's car. I wanted to spend as much time with my *bodyguard* as possible.

Warmth enveloped me as Jax draped his suit jacket over my shoulders and wound his arms around me from behind to button it. His scent clung to the material, and I decided it was now my favorite smell. I could breathe that in all night.

"You didn't need to do that."

"You were cold." His breath warmed my cheek. He lingered for a second more before letting me go. "Now I have an excuse to see you again."

Flirt back. Come on, you can do it. "You didn't need an excuse." Maybe I wasn't completely horrid at this after all.

He grinned, and I noticed he didn't have a toothpick anymore. Reaching for the car door, he opened it. "Good night, Bryer."

I slid into the passenger seat, and Jax closed the door, waiting for Dani to put the car in reverse.

"What the hell, Bry? You can't just go walking around with strange guys at night!" Dani revved the engine and sped off. "I was ready to jump out and—"

"And what?" I interrupted, annoyed that he was acting so overprotective. "You'd what, Dani? Beat him up? Go to jail?"

His grip on the steering wheel tightened. "Bry, you know I'd do whatever I can for you. But you have to be smart. What if I'm not around?"

I pulled Jax's jacket around me tighter and snuggled into it, leaning my head against the window. "For once, I wasn't afraid."

Dani's shoulders dropped. "Not everyone is bad."

"I hope not." I smiled into the collar. "I even flirted."

"You did not." He laughed.

I giggled. Clearly, my body was over-tired. "I did. And you know what?"

"What?" Dani looked over at me.

"He wants to see me again."

I didn't remember getting home. Or going to bed. But I woke with my alarm and tried to figure out which would be worse: having to get up or going back to sleep and having Rick's wrath fall down upon me for missing my shift.

Flinging back the covers, I knew which was worse, and if I didn't get up, I'd fall back to sleep. I was still wrapped in Jax's jacket but desperately needed a shower to wake up. I breathed in deeply, loving how I could smell him. I still couldn't believe he gave me his jacket. Tucking my nose into the fabric, I let myself pretend for a moment that he was there with me. That he wanted to be there.

It was a delusional fairytale dream, but still, I could fantasize for another minute before reality came crashing down.

The hot water for the shower wouldn't last long. I had the world's smallest water heater and had to choose between shaving or washing my hair—never both. And it certainly wasn't long enough for me to let my fingers linger while thinking of Jax.

27

But my mind went to *'what if,'* and my body was hyper-aware of every touch. Damn loofa.

I rinsed off and jumped out before my teeth started chattering. My messy bun was only damp from the water spray, but my legs were smooth. Priorities. I couldn't feel pretty if I had prickly cactus legs under my jeans.

And after last night, I wanted to apply some time towards my appearance, just in case. I mean, Jax could show up looking for his jacket. He'd want it back at some point. Wouldn't he?

Putting in my contacts, I realized I was proud of 'last-night-me' for at least remembering to take them out before falling asleep. Having contacts stuck to my eyes didn't sound appealing. Blinking, the mirror came back into focus. I didn't have horrible eyesight, but I hated the fuzziness. I could see a picture across the room. I could even tell there were people in it. Just don't ask me to identify who they are because I couldn't see the details.

I rummaged around my tiny makeup bag that held more space than essentials. Mascara, dollar store lash curler, and lightly tinged lip gloss looked to be the only thing that wasn't broken, empty, or so old I should probably toss them out.

Attempting to curl my lashes was nearly an impossible feat. I was cursed with straight lashes that twisted in ugly clumps and hated to be lifted. If I was lucky, I'd get them to last an hour.

Sighing, I backed away from the sink and grabbed my clothes. Looking at the clock, I cursed. I had less than twenty minutes to get to the restaurant, and my car was still across town.

"Shit. Shit. Shit. Shit." I tugged on my shoes and grabbed my keys. If I left now and ran, I might make it. I was halfway down the rickety stairs over the garage when I remembered the jacket. Rushing back, I fumbled with the keys and dropped them. The clink of the metal hitting the cement underneath made my heart stop. "No. No, no, no, nooooo."

Crying wasn't an option after having applied mascara. It's okay. I can climb down there, get the keys, and return for the jacket. I could still do this.

Using my phone's flashlight, I looked for the keys while crawling under the stairs. "Where in the hell did they go?" I breathed out heavily. A glint off my car key with fake diamond studs set in silicone glared back at me from just between the foundation crack of the garage and the ground. "You've got to be kidding me."

If this was how the day was going to go, I was screwed. At least it wasn't my phone. It already had so many cracks it couldn't afford another one. Sitting back on my heels, I contemplated my choices. Headlights filled the drive as a car pulled in. I tensed and forced myself to not throw up. My heart raced as I panicked, thinking it was Rick.

"What are you doing down there?" Dani's worried but quiet voice filled the space between us as he exited his car.

I gripped my shirt over my heart and slumped against the side of the garage. "Oh, thank God."

"Bry," he whispered, crouching next to me. "Seriously, what are you doing?" Concern etched his face, and the shadows created by the headlights almost made him look menacing. I couldn't see him as anything other than my brother, but I could see why others might fear him.

"I dropped my keys. What are *you* doing here?" I was surprised to see him so early in the morning, especially after waiting for me so late last night.

"I couldn't sleep, and the thought of some guy picking you up and kidnapping you while you walked to work pissed me off." He shrugged. "So here I am."

I gave a half-hearted chuckle. "I think the term is ladynapped. I'm not a kid." I meant it as a joke, but the look on his face told me he didn't take it that way.

"Even more of a reason to make sure you make it to work safely."

"Well, I can't get kidnapped or anything else until I get my keys." I pointed to the crack holding my keyring hostage.

Dani ground his teeth but didn't say anything. He got up and walked back to his car.

"Hey, where are you going?" I called out in the loudest whisper I could without waking Rick or my mother.

He stalked back with a wire hanger. "Getting your keys."

I smiled sweetly. "Thank you."

He snagged the keyring and pulled it out. I grabbed them quickly and flung my arms around his neck, squealing. "Thank you, thank you, thank you!"

Releasing him, I jogged up the stairs and unlocked my door to snatch Jax's jacket. Holding it close to my chest, I made sure not to drop it or my keys as I rushed to Dani's car.

He took one look at the jacket and shook his head. "Really?"

"What? He could come back for it, and I don't want to not have it with me." And... if I slipped it on now, there might be enough of his scent left to cling to me for the rest of the day.

Slipping it on, I wrapped it around me and inhaled deeply.

Dani grumbled something about strange men but mainly drove in silence. I was grateful. I wasn't ready to break my fantasy, and talking about it with him would do just that.

We pulled up to the restaurant with three minutes to spare. "Thank you for the ride."

He stuck out his hand. "Give me your car key so I can fix your tire and bring you your car."

"Unfortunately, I don't have the moo-la to fix it." I shrugged. "It will just have to stay there until the city tows it."

He rolled his eyes, something he's done since we were kids. "I didn't ask if you had money, Bry."

"I can't keep relying on you to fix everything. One day I'm gonna have to fall on my ass and find a way to pick myself back up."

"You've already been pushed on your ass more times than I can count. Shit, you've had more holes to dig yourself out of than the average prairie dog."

I feigned a gasp. "Are you calling me a dog?"

"You know what I mean. For once… I want to see you on top. I want to know you're okay and someone can look after you the way you deserve. Do you understand?"

I hated it when he turned all sweet. It made me uncomfortable. It reminded me of all my vulnerabilities and how often he'd seen them. "Maybe one day that will happen, but today… I just need to open the restaurant and make some tips. Today, I want to pretend that the guy who gave me this jacket is real, and for a moment, I just want to be a woman who was hit on by a man who didn't want to hurt me. I want to go in there," I gestured to Silversmith's, "and not think about whatever hole I'm in. Do *you* understand?" I wasn't gonna say anything about Jax, but Dani was my best friend. He knew me better than anyone. And I wanted to tell *someone*.

He turned in his seat and took my hands. "Bry. Not all men want to hurt women." He ground his jaw. "I hate that this is even a conversation between us. But shit, you know better than anyone how bad some can be. I just want you to be careful."

"That's all I ever am," I barely whispered. Careful. Watchful. Tense. Cautious. Suspicious. I'm a freaking thesaurus for alert. But never have I been reckless or trusting.

Yet… Jax gave me that, even if only for one night, I *felt* it. It was a small glimmer of hope that maybe, just maybe, I would find my fairytale ending. I'd never get a knight on a white horse, but I didn't want that. I wanted love. *Real* love. And safety.

Last night, when Jax wrapped his arms around me to give me his jacket, it was like the world couldn't get to me. Like I was protected, and there wasn't a soul who could reach me without going through him first.

It was stupid. I knew that but wanted to cling to the dream a bit longer.

I slipped my car key off and handed it over to Dani. "Thank you. You're the best."

He flashed me one of his toothy grins. "Yeah, yeah… set me up with that cute redhead who works the morning shift, and we can call us even. Tell *her* how great I am."

"I don't know. Her boyfriend might be opposed to her having a date with you." I wasn't sure Alice had a guy, but it was fun to watch Dani squirm. "Kidding. I'll see what I can do."

He leaned over and gripped the handle, shoving the door open. "Get to work. I'll bring your car by later."

I laughed all the way to the doors. I'm not sure how I would have gone through life without Dani. He deserved happiness. If he wanted a date, I would try everything to make it happen. Now… to see if Alice was on the schedule to work today.

Chapter 6

Jax

I tapped the truck's steering wheel before grabbing a box of toothpicks from the glove compartment. I slid a new one between my teeth, instantly comforted by the familiar taste and texture.

Shit. I was a mess. Not for the first time, I contemplated how early was *too early* to show up at the restaurant to see Bryer.

I'd spent the night dreaming of her. But it wasn't exactly peaceful. We were in a war zone, and I had to protect her, save her... and I woke unsure if I did. It rattled me to my core. I tried to fall back to sleep but then dreamed she was among a group of girls caught in a trafficking ring, and I woke with bile rising in my throat.

Watching the sunrise without anyone around me felt like the only place I could reassure myself they were just dreams. Sitting in the truck, I was alone with my thoughts, and every single one went to Bryer.

I'd traced her body in my mind so many times I memorized every curve. Her smile was now a core memory that would be the last thing I saw before my last breath. I could become deaf and still hear her voice... her laugh.

I hadn't believed in love at first sight, but damn if it didn't feel that way. I was almost forty years old, and my heart began beating for the first time last night.

Headlights bounced up the drive, and I squinted in the early dawn to see one of our ranch trucks sneaking home. My lip twitched into a grin as I twirled the toothpick over my tongue. This should be good. Fox was the only one who didn't come home last night.

As the youngest of our brotherhood, he was subject to more shit than the others. I wondered how long it would take him to realize I was out here, watching.

Shutting the truck off, Fox let it roll up the drive. I chuckled. He thought he could sneak in. I waited, allowing him to head for the bunkhouse before I opened my door. "Hey, brother."

He stopped, stiffening before turning on his heel and slumping his shoulders. He ambled over to my truck and slipped into the passenger seat. "It's not what you think."

"It's after six in the morning, and you're just getting home. That's not true?" I loved fucking with him.

"Well, yeah, but..."

I tapped the steering wheel. "You were with a girl."

"Yes, but it isn't what you think."

I laughed. "Fox, listen. We don't care as long as you're good to her."

He crinkled his nose and shook his head. "It's not like that. We talked. She's sweet and innocent. Nothing like..."

"Nothing like the girls we find." I understood that all too well. I had spent an entire night thinking about a girl who I prayed would never be in a situation like those we saved.

He nodded. "It was refreshing to just talk to someone without the weight of the world pressing down. You know?" He shook his head. "She's different."

Mmhm. "And you like her."

"No. I mean, yeah, but not like that. But I think we could be friends."

"Friends." I drawled out the word as if testing it for him.

"Come on." His groan filled the cab. "It's late, and I'm tired. Can we talk about this after I get a nap?"

I laughed again. "First, it's early, not late. The sun is already poking over the mountain. Second, there's no time for a nap. Diesel called a meeting while you were *talking* last night. Everyone to the main house by seven."

He slumped in the seat and grumbled. "It's gonna be a long day."

I slapped a hand on his shoulder. "You ain't kidding." I was already counting down the hours and minutes until I could leave to find Bryer. "Let's go get some coffee in you. Wake you right up."

I wasn't sure who would be up first fighting for control of the kitchen... Maria or Flapjack. But either way, there'd be coffee.

We walked toward the house. Fox paused before squinting at the truck, then at me. "So why are *you* still up?"

"Someone had to make sure you got home." There was no way in hell I would tell him I had nightmares about my beautiful angel and failed to save her.

"Psh, that's some bullcrap." He trudged behind me, giving one longing look over his shoulder to the bunkhouse where his bed probably called to him. "I'm not a kid. I don't need a damn babysitter."

Hearing him curse was still odd and slightly funny. I wasn't sure I could take him seriously. At twenty-one years old, he had been with us for almost three years and was still drying out behind the ears.

Inside, the main house was toasty warm, with a fire crackling in the fireplace. Maria's husband, Lupe, sat at the bar overlooking the kitchen, shaking his head and chuckling. "Buenos días. If you are looking for coffee, you should take a seat. It might be a while."

He wore his usual red and black checkered long-sleeved shirt, and his tattered old cowboy hat, which used to be white but was now more of a tanned faded color, sat resting on his knee. His withered dark skin wrinkled when he smiled, watching the unfolding events in the kitchen. Maria was his world. That woman could do no wrong in his eyes.

After their daughter was sold into trafficking, Jacob tried to find her, but it was too late. He returned to Lupe and Maria empty-handed but was embraced as a son, and we've all been family ever since. It was hard to think back to when I was with another family. My blood family.

It was hard to shake off the overwhelming feeling of grief that attempted to consume me whenever I remembered my mother and sister crying over my grave. I had been there, standing at my own funeral, watching from afar, ensuring no one hurt them while they said their goodbyes. It was the only way to protect them. Leaving was hard, but knowing they would have died because of me...

My death was the only way for them to live.

And I'd do it again. No regrets.

Diesel came in from the back office and clamped a hand down on my shoulder. "Morning." He offered a shit-eating grin and gripped my shoulder tighter. "You got in late."

Fox laughed, taking a seat at the long dining table. "He was with a girl."

Bear strolled in, yawning as he grabbed a seat next to Fox. "Who was with a girl?"

Fox knocked on the table and gave a toothy grin. "Jax."

Bear's brow furrowed. "Yeah, we were both with her."

Lupe nearly choked as he spun on his barstool to face the room. "Maybe some things should be left behind doors, eh' mijo?"

Bear looked confused for half a second before he realized his mistake. "Shit, that's not what I meant. You should all get your heads examined. They're always in the gutter." He groaned. "Where's the coffee? A man needs something more than water to deal with all you asshats this early in the morning."

Diesel leaned over the counter where Flapjack and Maria were arguing over who would cook. "I don't give a flying fuck what you fix for breakfast, but if you don't get some coffee out here, you're gonna have to deal with Sam. I ain't afraid to sick her on you both."

Samantha was trained as a personal assassin for the cartel. Diesel couldn't have found a better partner.

Flapjack slapped a kitchen towel on the counter. "Tell Maria to get out of my kitchen, and I'll gladly fix the entire county a fucking cup of coffee."

Maria rolled her eyes and continued to make tortillas. "You love my cooking."

I picked up the discarded towel and threw it at Flapjack. "Face it, you're not gonna win. Might as well take a seat and retire your apron. Let us have the coffee, man. We're dying here."

Maria leaned over the counter and touched my cheek. "You can have the first cup."

"Maria, you sure know how to make a guy feel special." I looked over at Lupe. "If you ever tire of her..."

"Not a chance." He laughed. "Wife, stop teasing the young men and give me a kiss before one of them steals you away from me!"

She scurried around the corner to give him a quick kiss. "I could never resist you."

He playfully gave her butt a pat as she left. An almost remorseful glint seeped through his smile as he watched her. He had come so close to losing her just months before to a bullet in her chest. It was the final straw before Jacob demanded they return to the States with us. He was securing their visas and doing all he could to ensure they remained with us in Nevada.

Sam and Callie came into the house together, lost in their conversation.

Diesel pulled out a chair at the table for Sam before taking his seat. "Well, it looks like everyone is here. I guess it's time to start the meeting."

"Without coffee?" Bear scoffed. "This ain't gonna end well."

Sam stopped in her tracks and narrowed her glare on Flapjack. "No coffee?"

He raised his hands in defense. "Why are you looking at me like it's my fault?"

She placed her hands on her hips. "Is it not *your* kitchen?"

"Not anymore." He took Callie's hand and brought it to his lips before tugging her to his lap. "Apparently, no one cares if I'm demoted."

"You hush in there!" Maria came around the corner carrying a carafe. "You have more important things to do than feed this family." She winked at Flapjack as she poured me the first cup of coffee.

Diesel chuckled and took the carafe from her to fill his mug, then Sam's. "She's right. And, I think that officially starts the meeting." He took a sip of coffee and coughed. "But maybe we should let Flapjack stay in charge of the morning fuel."

Maria batted at him with her apron. "You need something stronger than brown water."

Callie flashed Flapjack a smile and held her cup up to be filled. "I actually prefer mine to be cream-colored." She would probably prefer ice and some kind of pumpkin flavoring too.

"Alright, guys. Just because Jacob is gone on his honeymoon doesn't mean we stop working." Diesel looked down the table to Bear and then me. "We have a security detail that I need one of you to take care of."

"You mean you need a babysitter." Bear folded his arms and leaned back in his seat.

"A bodyguard," Diesel countered.

Bear huffed. "Is there a difference?"

Security details were the least favorite part of our jobs. Throw us into a pit of venomous snakes, surround us with a cartel of trigger-happy assholes, send us into a terrorist-ridden city for an extraction, and we are happy. But saddle us with a holier-than-thou millionaire, and nine out of ten times, that's exactly who we ended up guarding, and we're like little kids whining about having to do a fucking chore.

"Then why the fuck are you looking at me?" Bear gestured at me. "Why not him?"

Diesel took a drink and grimaced at the coffee. "Look, I don't give a shit which one of you does it, but Fox hasn't been trained enough to handle this particular client, and Flapjack needs to stay here to help me."

Flapjack laughed. "Seniority is a bitch, isn't it, gentlemen."

"Fuck you." Bear flipped him off.

With a shrug, Flapjack laughed more. "You could always rock, paper, scissor it."

No way in hell was I going on a detail. I had other plans. Plans that involved a certain brown-haired woman. "I have to check in with Ana's. Not sure I'll have time." It wasn't a lie. It was my job to ensure Ana's Place was running smoothly. I checked in with Tressa once a month. She was our longest live-in, who now ran it for us.

Ana's Place was the sanctuary Jacob had constructed not long after meeting Lupe and Maria. He even named it after their daughter.

"Bullshit." Bear readied his hands into the formal 'rock' position.

"You're serious?" I raised a brow and bit down on my toothpick.

He held his hands up, ready to play. "Got a better idea?"

I sat my mug down and let the toothpick roll over my tongue. "I can't believe I'm doing this." I was damn near forty years old and playing a kid's game. If I lost, I was gonna be pissed.

Flapjack tapped the table. "Best two out of three. I'll judge."

I glared at him. As if we needed his supervision. Shriveled, unuseful prick. I turned my attention to Bear. "You fucking cheat, and I'll make sure you die a slow, painful death."

Bear smirked. "I may be a lot of things, but a cheat ain't one of them."

Rock, paper, scissors... rock. I clenched the toothpick as I grinned victoriously.

Bear readied his hands for another round. "Look at that shit-eating grin. A little premature, don't ya think? But then again, that might be a thing for you."

"Ouch. That's brutal." Fox leaned with his elbows on the table, completely invested in our competition.

Sucking in a deep breath, I shrugged. "Funny, I swore that's what your hand said last night. You know... those walls are awfully thin."

Bear let out a sarcastic laugh. "Hardy har har."

Rock, paper, scissors... scissors. Damn it.

Bear smashed his 'rock' over my hand. "Rock, bitch!"

39

"Alright, last one." Flapjack continued his self-appointed management of our game. "Whoever loses this one gets the security detail."

Bear and I both glared at him before continuing.

Rock, paper, scissors... paper.

Thank God.

Every muscle I had relaxed. "I guess you and your hand will have plenty of time to work on that *premature thing* while you're babysitting."

"Fuck you." He grumbled and grabbed his coffee. "Alright, so tell me, how bad is this gonna hurt?"

Diesel chuckled. "Depends on if you use lube or not."

Fox kicked back in his seat, chuckling. Even Lupe had a toothy grin.

Bear hollered over his shoulder, "Maria, I'm gonna need something stronger to start this day!"

Diesel draped his arm over the back of Sam's chair and whispered something in her ear that made her blush. With a smirk, he sat up straighter. "Her name is Hailey Albrecht, and her father is..."

Bear tensed, sitting up with more focus. "Garrett fucking Albrecht. CEO of Albrecht Internationals."

Diesel nodded. "That's the guy. He's been all over the news the last few years. Apparently, he needs certain information to disappear, and he made a contract selling his daughter to someone who claims they can do just that."

"So now he wants to hide his daughter? Fucking asshole. He should've protected his family when he had the chance. Sniveling coward. He shouldn't be allowed near this girl after selling her." Bear clenched his jaw. "I ain't okay with hand delivering her back to the fucker."

"Actually, she hired us herself." A smug grin lifted Diesel's upper lip. "She didn't know about the shady dealings her father was involved in and is completely innocent. She happened to overhear the conversation and his deal to hand her over in return for a clean slate. She escaped and found a way to the safe house in Michigan."

"Callie's?" I asked, wanting to clarify. Jacob had a few safe houses.

Callie nodded. "Yeah. I don't know how she found it, but I'm glad she did. Carter's dad called us immediately."

"That's messed up. Her own dad selling her." Fox hung his head. "Some people don't deserve kids."

He wasn't wrong. Coffee discarded, we all focused on the newest mission. "Who did Garrett Albrecht make a deal with?"

Diesel sobered, and I knew the answer wouldn't be good. "Bandito."

The room went so quiet only the steady hum of the fireplace fan could be heard. Flapjack paled and gripped Callie tighter. We all had our own vendetta against Bandito, but Carter more than the rest of us. After being held on Bandito's private island, he carried his own internal scars that needed the soothing balm of revenge.

Bear stared off, his thoughts intensely fixated on his detail. "I'm assuming she knows *who* might be after her since she ran?"

Diesel nodded again.

"Well, shit." Bear took the last swig of his coffee. "You sure just one of us is enough?"

"You know we don't do solo missions." Diesel got up, walked to the office, and returned with a manilla folder and a box. He handed Bear the folder. "Wes will meet you at the airport. He'll be your pilot for this trip... and your second. You'll be taking Ms. Albrecht together to the safe house in Idaho. Jacob will meet you there and decide who else will be needed to ensure her safety around the clock." He paused. "It was always gonna be you, Bear. You're exactly who Ms. Albrecht needs right now."

"Who's Wes?" Fox's brow pulled together as he absentmindedly rubbed his shoulder. Poor kid. He'd be living with a lifetime of pain from that gunshot wound. We all should know. I think all of us but Diesel had been shot at some point. Some of us more than once.

"He's a... hired gun," Diesel smirked. "He's also a damned good pilot, and Jacob has contracted him on a retainer. We've used him a few times."

Wes was definitely someone to keep on your good side. He was a sniper in the military. And, like me, he just wanted to disappear after his last tour, but he didn't stay here at the ranch with the rest of us. The last time we worked together was before we found Lily.

Bear pulled out the file on Hailey Albrecht. Paperclipped to the top was her picture. I had to fight back a laugh. Bear was gonna be in for a feisty trip. Redheads were never submissive.

He glowered over her history and whatever information was provided for her. His glare found its way to me. "You owe me."

"I won fair and square. I don't owe you shit." Chuckling, I gestured to the file. "Looks like fun."

"Yeah..." Bear exhaled. "When do I leave?"

"Wes should be at the airport by ten. You'll collect Ms. Albrecht and then fly with her to Idaho. And thanks to Callie talking Jacob into the twenty-first century, there's more in that envelope."

Bear pulled out a watch. "What the fuck is this?"

"I believe it's to tell time. Our ancestors used them before cellphones like a sundial you wear on your wrist." Fox smirked and took a drink of coffee.

"You're all a bunch of smartasses today, aren't you." Bear held the watch up. "I know WHAT it is. Why is it in here?"

"After what happened with Flapjack, we aren't taking any more chances with family. It has a tracker in it." Diesel placed the box on the table. "That brings me to the rest of this morning's business."

"There's more? Damn, today just keeps getting better." Bear shoved the papers back into the envelope.

"Kind of. Jacob decided to leave me to hand these out." He opened the box and handed Flapjack a watch. "We each have one."

Diesel lifted a smaller box and handed it to Sam. "I didn't think you'd want a watch. Jacob agreed to let the ladies have something more... feminine."

Sam opened hers, revealing a pair of diamond stud earrings. "Pretty *and* useful."

"Lily has a pair, and you too, Callie." Diesel handed Flapjack's wife her earrings. "After Panama, Jacob realized we needed to utilize technology to keep us safe."

I couldn't disagree. Not knowing where Flapjack had been taken weighed heavily on all of us. There wasn't a rock we wouldn't have overturned to find him, but a tracker would have been nice. "What's the range on these?"

Diesel returned to his seat. "These will give a precise location. Thanks to GPS, Wi-Fi, and cell tower triangulation, we will always know where you are... anywhere."

"Will it tell you when I'm taking a piss too?" Bear strapped the watch to his wrist.

I grabbed my box. "Just be glad it's not a fitness tracker. You'd have to use your other hand." Strapping the watch on, I checked the time. Almost eight.

Diesel intervened before Bear could curse me. "Jax, you said you have to visit Ana's. When are you leaving?"

Shit. I didn't want to leave until I could talk to Bryer. "Tomorrow. I have some things to take care of today."

"Does this have anything to do with a certain girl?" Bear kicked back and folded his arms.

I narrowed my stare on him. "Don't you have someplace to be?"

"Wait. A girl?" Callie sat up straighter and tapped Sam's arm. "Did you know about this?"

Sam shook her head. "No, but I'm intrigued."

I stood and twirled the toothpick over my tongue. "Ladies, you will continue to be intrigued because I have nothing to say."

"It is a girl!" Callie squealed. "Can we meet her?"

I dipped my head in a quick goodbye at Lupe and the others. "Don't check my tracker." I clamped a hand down on

Bear's shoulder as I passed him. "Shoot straight, stay safe. I'll see you soon."

Maria came around the corner carrying a platter of bacon and eggs. I snatched a crispy piece of meat. "You're the best."

Sneaking out was easier now that food had arrived. I was hungry, sure, but I'd rather starve than waste one more minute without seeing Bryer.

Chapter 7

Bryer

The clock teased me from over the bar. It was *only* nine o'clock. My shift was never going to end. I still had six hours left.

Alice hip-bumped me. "Hey, girl. Don't look, but a gorgeous man in booth seven is asking for *you* personally."

My heart hammered as I hoped it was my bodyguard. I spun around and was greeted with the warmest pair of chocolate-colored eyes. Sure thing, Jax sat in the booth, his gaze traveled lower, roaming over every inch of me, setting my body on fire.

Trembling, I pushed off the bar and walked toward him. I wasn't sure what to say first. Yet, he was like a magnet, drawing me in and forcing my quivering legs to move.

"Hi." *Hi?* I really sucked at flirting.

"Angel." His voice was as deep and raspy as I remembered it.

Breathe. I had to remember to breathe.

Oh, crap. He was probably here for his jacket, not me. I'm so stupid. "Um, I'll be right back."

Grabbing the jacket, I sniffed it, trying to memorize the intoxicating scent. It sucked I had to give it back so soon. I rushed out to where he waited. A concerned look pulled his brow together.

"Here," I said, handing it over. "Thank you again for letting me borrow it."

He didn't take it but instead sat there staring at me. "Did you bring another?"

"Coat? Oh, no. I'm fine." He didn't need to know about the worn-out hoodie I used for almost every occasion.

45

He shrugged off his Carhartt coat and handed it out to me. "Trade me then."

"I can't." This man had to be imaginary. A fictional illusion I made up to keep my sanity in this hell of a life.

Well, if I made him up, I guess I failed to keep my sanity.

"You can, and you will. What kind of man would I be if I let an angel freeze?"

Behind me, Alice let out an audible swoon. A blush warmed my cheeks. "Okay."

I traded him jackets, holding the new, heavier one close to my chest.

"Good girl." Jax shifted in the booth to face me, his knees almost touching mine. "What time do you get off?"

Breathe. "Three."

The ache between my legs intensified. I'd never been so turned on before. I wondered if last night was a fluke, but today was even stronger.

"Can I pick you up?" He twirled a toothpick with his tongue, and I was insanely jealous of the small piece of wood. I wondered how he kissed. What he tasted like.

Focus, Bryer. "Like a date? Just you and me?"

He smiled, and I swore the world flipped upside down. Holy crap. He gave a short nod. "Yeah."

If I didn't put some distance between us soon, I would be nothing more than a puddle on the floor that Alice would have to mop up. Okay, bad analogy. But it was true. I was a hot mess whenever I was around him. And I was now soaked in unmentionable areas. Not ideal for someone who still had almost an entire shift left at work.

I nodded. "Okay. Yes."

Alice squealed, and I glanced over my shoulder at her, giving her the best *shut-up* look I could manage. Jax chuckled and stood. He was at least a full head taller than me, but it was his closeness that I couldn't ignore. He removed his toothpick and leaned in. My chest grazed his as his mouth hovered near my ear.

"It might be a little soon for you to know this, but so help me, angel, you will be wearing this coat and in my truck at exactly three because I want the world to know you're mine."

His lips barely grazed my earlobe before he walked away. I stood there, unable to move.

Holy shit.

Did he just say that?

Breathe.

Alice ran over to me and squealed again. "Okay, who was that, and does he have a brother?" She sighed as she watched him through the picture windows. "I want one."

I hugged the coat close, taking in his scent. *Agh*, why did he smell so good? I ignored Alice and made it to the back to hang it up. I wasn't sure how I was supposed to continue working after *that*.

I want the world to know you're mine.

Yeah, there was no way I could focus on anything else.

I couldn't believe he was picking me up. I couldn't wait to tell Dani.

Pulling out my phone, I sent him a quick text.

Me: *Don't hurry with the car*
I have a ride

Dani: *???*

Me: ...

Dani: *Bry*

Me: *Jax is picking me up*

Dani: *Maybe we should do a background check first*

Me: *Not funny*

Dani: *I'm not laughing*
Just be safe

...

I'll have my phone on
Call if you need me

...

I'll beat his ass if he tries anything

I rolled my eyes and shoved the phone into my back pocket. Rounding the corner, I found Alice filling the salt and pepper shakers at the bar. She flashed a teasing smile my way.

I joined her, thankful it was a slow morning and we had only one table. "You know, you could be less obvious."

"Me? Girl, you're the one who had a six-foot sex god come in here and ask for you *by name*."

I nearly choked on air. "A sex god?"

Alice shrugged. "I have an incredible imagination."

"I'm sure you do." I screwed on a lid and grabbed another full jar. "You know... my friend, Dani, he's into you."

Alice stopped filling the jar and looked at me. "No, he's not."

"Yeah. I could give him your number?"

"Um..." It was the first time I'd ever heard Alice not have words. "I... What if he doesn't call?"

"He'll call." And if he didn't, I'd break his legs. Or something. But I couldn't see Dani breaking a woman's heart on purpose.

"Bryer!" Rick called from the office.

"Shit. When did he get here?" I finished screwing on another lid and wiped my hands on my apron.

Alice shrugged. "I don't know. I haven't seen him all day."

Rick was friendly to his employees. But Alice had her suspicions that I could neither confirm nor deny. It was safer if she didn't know the truth.

In the office, Rick had me close the door. Everything was always behind the secrecy of a door.

He sat at his desk. Piles of invoices and food orders littered the top, along with payroll records.

Barely glancing up at me, he continued to work. "I need you to work a double today. Liv called out."

Today? I was already living on two hours of sleep and dragging hard. But also, Jax was picking me up at three.

So help me, angel, you will be wearing this coat and in my truck at exactly three because I want the world to know you're mine.

"I can't." I wrung my hands together, hoping I wouldn't have to explain myself.

He stopped whatever he was doing and looked up. A dark shadow crossed his features. "Why?"

My tongue felt three times too big. "I have plans." Please don't press for more.

He scoffed, "Plans." Getting up, he slowly made his way around the desk. He was so close I could smell the alcohol from last night still on his breath. "Plans change."

I wanted to shrivel up into a ball on the floor and roll away. Whatever backbone I thought I had vanished. It didn't matter what I wanted. But would Jax be mad if I canceled and never want to see me again? I couldn't be upset with him if he walked away. I was nothing more than a small-town waitress with car problems.

"I understand, but—"

"No buts." Rick sneered and gripped my upper arms. "You're so ungrateful." He shoved me back, letting me go. "Spoiled little bitch. I gave you this job because no one wants you, and this is how you repay me? If you want to keep this job, your plans will change."

My eyes burned as tears threatened to spill. I willed my body to hold back until I was away from him. I hated letting him know how he affected me. "I'm not trying to be ungrateful."

Scoffing, he returned to his seat behind the desk. "One more thing." He waved a white envelope. "I'm keeping your paycheck. You're behind on this month's rent, and I can't wait any longer."

My mouth fell open, but no words came out. I needed that money.

He smirked. "See? You need to work a few doubles to make next month's rent on time."

Bastard.

"Don't you have a job to do? Standing around here isn't going to make a paycheck." He shooed me away like I was a fly too close to his desk.

Fucking prick.

Asshole.

I balled my fists at my sides and turned on my heels to escape.

"Oh, and Bryer?"

I paused, staring at the door. I was so close.

"This stays between us. All my other employees would be upset to know you were treated with favoritism. It wouldn't look good if they knew I gave you all the extra shifts."

Cocksucker.

I didn't breathe again until I was in the hall with the office door shut firmly behind me. Slumping against the wall, I wanted to let the dark shadows swallow me whole.

Jax's coat taunted me from the employee rack. The tears I'd been holding back fell in torrents. I ran to the restroom and locked myself in a stall.

I couldn't breathe. The tears turned into hyperventilating sobs. I doubled over and wrapped my arms around my middle.

Years of frustration came out in a strangled cry. I have lived through worse; I could live through this. It was just a change of plans. It wasn't like I had a real shot with Jax anyway.

Life wasn't fair.

I sucked in a shaky breath and tried to calm down. Exiting the stall, I grabbed a handful of paper towels and blew my nose.

The door opened, and I immediately plastered on a fake smile that I hoped passed as happy.

"You okay?" Alice made sure the door shut and locked behind her.

"Yeah." I was a bit too bubbly and needed to tone it down. "Yeah. I'm fine." I smiled again for good measure. "I just got offered to pull a double." I dabbed at my nose and tried to covertly wipe away any remaining tears. "It's good too. I could really use it."

Alice clenched her jaw. "No."

"No?" I hiccoughed. I really needed to pull myself together.

"No. You can't pull a double. You have a date with the sex god, and you are not missing it." She flung an arm over my shoulder and pulled me in. "Just tell Rick no."

Easy for her to say. "I can't. I have rent due soon. Even with tips, I won't have enough. I'm screwed if I don't pull a few more doubles."

"That's bullshit. No offense, but your parents are jerks. I can't believe they charge you so much for that tiny place and won't give you any grace when you're short. They know what you make. They sign the paychecks." Her face lit up. "I've got it. Move in with me! No rent for three months, so you can start saving and get on your feet. I don't know why I haven't thought of this sooner." She hugged me closer and shook me as if she was half maraca. "Ahhh…. This will be so much fun!"

"I don't know." The idea of leaving my tiny apartment over Rick and my mom's garage both excited me and sent a spear of fear through me.

"Well, luckily for you, I do know." She stepped back, apparently pleased with her decision and gave me the world's biggest smile in the mirror. "Now, you'll go on your date and enjoy every minute. I will cover for you. Then… we'll pack your stuff up and start moving you in with me. It's not up for debate." Her smile softened, and I tried not to look at my reflection. "You deserve better, Bryer. And that man who could probably make all the panties in the county fall by just breathing wants to see *you*. You're going."

I sucked in another shaky breath and wiped a rogue tear away. "Thank you."

My heart felt a smidgen lighter. I was going on a date and then moving in with Alice. Maybe. My gut twisted in uncertainty. It didn't matter that I was an adult, Rick scared the living crap

51

out of me, and I wasn't sure how my new plans would make him react.

Chapter 8
Jax

Three o'clock couldn't come fast enough.

Two fifty-seven.

I parked as close to the front entrance as possible. My hands were sweating. My chest felt tight. Dear God... was I having a heart attack? Shit. What was I doing? I had to be at least double Bryer's age.

I needed to decide right now if I would let something like age bother me. She hadn't seemed fazed by it. But then again, she didn't know how much of a gap there might be between us.

I had three minutes to decide. After that, I would live with whatever decision I made. Looking through the front picture windows, I caught sight of Bryer. She hugged her friend and gave her a smile that I would burn the world down to see again.

Fuck it. A few years would not be an issue for me. I wouldn't let something as inane as age stop me from the one good thing God might have placed on this earth for me.

Exactly three o'clock.

The front doors opened, and she stepped outside, squinting under the late afternoon sun. She wore my coat, and damn if that didn't turn me on. A beast within me roared to life, wanting to make a predatory claim on her. I needed every man who breathed to know she was mine. That was some caveman shit, but damn, if it wasn't in my blood, screaming at me to do it.

I jumped out and met her at the curb.

Her gaze flicked over me, but she quickly looked away with the deepest blush across her cheeks. "I wasn't sure you'd actually show."

"Angel, when I say I'm gonna do something, I mean it." I opened the truck's passenger door for her and held my hand out to help her inside. It was like electricity when we touched. Not in some mumbo jumbo voodoo way, but like in a heavy attraction, I could touch this woman all day and night and never be enough kind of way. It was an unmistakable yet satisfying feeling, knowing I was an addict, and she was my drug. One touch is all it took for me to be lost to her.

Climbing into the driver's seat, I looked over at her. Fuck, she was gorgeous. She had stray strands of hair that had fallen from her messy bun, and a small grease stain adorned the left side of her shirt. But nothing could diminish her beauty. "You look good as my passenger princess."

The crimson blush deepened across her face. She began shrugging out of my coat, and my heart dropped. No. I didn't want it back. I wanted her in it until her scent was woven into the fabric.

I placed my hand on her arm. "Baby girl, it's still chilly out."

"I can't keep your coat. What would you wear?"

Shit. Right now, I was so fucking hot that there was no way I'd need a coat as long as she was around. "Trust me. I don't need it."

She pulled the coat closer and snuggled in. *Good girl.*

I pulled away from the restaurant and headed toward the river. It had been forever since I'd been on a date, and I wanted to do it right. I wanted a place where we could talk, but I didn't want to do something as average as just dinner. Food would be later tonight.

"So… where are we going?" She looked as scared as a baby deer caught in the headlights. Her eyes widened, and she twisted her hands together on her lap. She broke out in a full-body shiver, and I worried there was more behind her fear than she let on. She didn't know what I did for a living or how I could pick up on tics. She also didn't know I had a special knack for calming people.

I reached over and laced my fingers with hers, bringing her hand to my leg. Instantly, she stopped trembling.

I grinned, turning down the frontage road. "What's going on in that pretty little head?"

"You'll think I'm stupid." She ducked.

"Hey, I told you, your worth is not on the ground. Look up, angel." I waited for her to do as I said. "I promise you, I don't think you're stupid."

She huffed a small scoff that was almost a laugh. "I just thought... I don't know you, and I got in your truck and... I was scared."

"You're right to be afraid. There are some sick people out there who would do horrible things to you." I brought her hand to my lips, where I kissed her knuckles. "But there is no world in which I would hurt you."

"That's what they all say." Her chest picked up, and I knew if I didn't do something soon, she might go into a full panic.

I pulled the truck over and placed it into park. Turning to face her, I kept her hand tightly in mine. "Bryer, look at me."

Her eyes fluttered innocently as she did as I requested. Such an obedient girl. I wasn't sure if I wanted to praise her or punish her for it. "I'm not gonna lie to you because I believe all relationships are built on trust."

She took a steadying breath. Softly, she chewed on her bottom lip, and I wanted to take her lip between my teeth and suck. Fuck. Focus man.

Holding her hand, I caressed her soft skin with my thumb. "I'm not a good man. I've seen and done things that would give a good man nightmares. But I will not ever hurt a woman. I promise you, nowhere is safer than when you're with me."

I knew it was a promise I'd keep because, in the short time since I'd met her, I'd been ready to scorch the earth and collapse civilizations just to be with her. Even my dreams were centered around sacrificing everything, even my life, to save her.

She swallowed hard, but she didn't try to pull away. "What does that mean? What have you done?"

"Everything."

Her breath hitched. "Killed?" The tiny squeak in her voice destroyed me.

"Yes." But please don't ask me how many times. I lost count years ago.

Her chest rose quickly, and she tugged on her hand, but not enough to actually want to be released, so I held on. I couldn't lose her yet.

"What about rape?"

I shook my head. "No. I told you, I won't hurt a woman. Besides, I have no reason to force a woman to have sex with me."

She tightened her grip on my hand. That was a good sign.

"Have you kidnapped anyone?"

I offered a half chuckle. "Not a woman."

Her shoulders relaxed, and she peered more intently at me. "Torture?"

"Yes." I didn't think she was gonna ask more after she found out I killed someone. But she was giving me hope with every question. Maybe she wouldn't be afraid.

Her mouth twisted to the side. "But not a woman."

I shook my head. "No."

There was a brief pause where she relaxed even more. Her thumb now grazing my fingers. "Are you in the mafia?"

I laughed. I couldn't help it. I loved how her mind tracked everything to that question. She was smart and to the point. "It feels like it some days. But no. I'm more of a mercenary. Kind of. Hell, I don't know if there's a word for whatever I am."

A lift of her lip made my heart race. Her head cocked slightly as she took me in. "Vigilante."

"A ghost."

Her smile widened. "So… security."

I laughed again. "Yeah, security."

"Well, Mr. Jax, you are a bouquet of red flags. I should probably ask you to take me back to the restaurant." She turned in her seat but was now back to her semi-confident self. We needed to work on that. There was no reason for her to ever doubt herself. "But I think your red flags are my green ones. I can't explain it, but I trust you." She gave me a playful side-eyed grin. "One more question."

"Angel, you can ask as many as you want."

"How old are you?"

I laughed. That was not what I thought would be next. It seemed so mundane after asking if I was a murderer. "Almost forty."

Her fingers ticked off years. "That's only... seventeen years difference."

I put the truck into drive and continued toward the river. "I know it's a bit of a gap, but I've already decided I don't care."

"I just decided I don't care either." She was so cute, *just deciding*.

We made it to the river on the south side of town and parked. I jumped out and barely reached the other side before Bryer got out. Gripping her waist, I lifted her from the truck. "Rule one: I always open your doors."

"I'm completely capable of opening a door. I don't want you to go out of your way for me."

I kept my hands at her waist. "I know you are capable. It isn't to diminish the independent woman in you, but there are two reasons. The first is to give me time to ensure the area is safe enough for my queen to enter."

She swallowed hard. Her breathing nearly stopped. "And the second?"

"Is a selfish reason." I pulled her to me, so we were flush. "Not only can I guard you with my body, but I get to touch you."

From here, I could see her heartbeat racing in her neck. The steady thump matched mine.

She took a step back. "I'm hardly a queen. You shouldn't worry so much."

"On the contrary, you are a queen... and I already told you, you're mine. So yes, I will worry. It's my job to make sure you are safe."

She chuckled. "Like a personal bodyguard."

"Baby girl, I will be so much more than that." I pulled a blanket from the back of the cab and tucked it under my arm before grabbing her hand.

I had scoured the area earlier, looking for the perfect spot. This one had a few trees for cover, but the water wasn't far away, giving a tranquil sound. It was perfect for talking.

I spread the blanket over the ground. Sitting, I gestured for her to join me.

She hesitated for a moment before sitting. Wrapping her arms around her knees, she watched me. My coat still hung on her like a thick blanket. "Have you really killed someone?"

"I have."

"Do you regret it?"

I shook my head. "No. I mean... there's one I regret, but the rest deserved everything they got."

Her eyes widened. "There's more than one?"

I dug a toothpick out of my pocket and clenched it tightly between my teeth. "It's kind of unavoidable in my line of work."

"Tell me about it."

"Bryer... I want to be honest with you, but I'm not sure that's a good idea."

"I have lived with monsters my entire life. I need to decide if you're a good or bad one."

What the fuck did she mean she's lived with monsters her whole life? "Your answer may very well be hiding in the reaction I will give when you answer *my* question. Has someone hurt you?"

She looked away, chewing on her lip again. "It's pretty here. I've never been down to the river."

"You're purposely avoiding my question."

She turned back, flashing me a fucking fake smile. "I'm giving you a compliment. Thank you for bringing me here."

"No, you're trying to de-escalate something you think is blowing up. I promised you I wouldn't hurt you. My anger is not, nor will it ever be at you. You said you've lived with monsters your entire life. Has someone hurt you?"

"I'm fine. Please, let's talk about something else. I don't want to ruin this day."

"You want to know more about what I do. That's fair." Maybe she would trust me enough to tell me her secrets. Tell me who her monsters are. "I kidnap, torture, and kill assholes who hurt women and children. I rescue people who have been trafficked. I walk into the evilest parts of the world and demand revenge for those who can't. I see what happens to those who've been abused in every way, and I die a little. So, yes, baby girl, when I ask you about the monsters in your life, and I see the hesitant response in your eyes, I know you see a devil in mine because I would do vile things to anyone who ever hurt you."

She inched closer to me. "The scary thing is... I don't see a devil at all."

I smirked. "Beauty never saw the Beast either. Didn't mean he wasn't one."

"If you're trying to convince me to leave, you're doing a poor job. That happens to be my favorite fairytale."

"You know it's Stockholm Syndrome, right? She was his captive."

Bryer shrugged. "I don't see it that way. I don't care what the world sees."

Now I was even more curious. "What do you see?"

Her features softened as she lost herself in thought. "I see a young woman who never imagined anyone could love her for her. A man who was so lost in his wrongdoings that he became what he wanted the world to believe he was. But they saw each other. It was the truest love in any fairytale. He was willing to sacrifice himself to save her. I think that's the ultimate level of swoon."

"There's levels of swoon?" I chuckled.

She swatted at my arm. "Yes. Don't make fun of me. It's my fairytale."

I leaned in to touch her face. "Do I make you swoon?"

"Yes, but not on Beast's level. He fought off a rabid pack of wolves for Beauty."

"So that's the bar you've set for me. Wolves?"

She blinked and looked up at me through her lashes. "No. The bar I set for you is much lower."

"Oh?"

Her breathing quickened. "It all rides on a kiss."

"You afraid I won't know what I'm doing?" I traced her lips with my fingertips, loving how she quivered.

She shook her head. "I'm scared to death you'll hate how inexperienced I am and not want to fight the wolves for me after all."

Fuck me. Inexperienced? There is no way in hell this woman hasn't been kissed properly by a man. But damn, if that didn't make my cock throb. "Angel, I'm about to wage war with every wolf in the world for you."

"What if the wolves are monsters?"

"I'll kill them all." Sliding my hand behind her head, I pulled her to me and sealed my mouth to hers. Fire and electricity mixed together as I caressed her tender lips.

She grabbed my shirt as I pressed my tongue lightly, begging her to open up and let me taste. Her lips parted, and I wasted no time slipping my tongue over hers. I wanted to dive into her and savor every inch.

I gripped her waist and yanked her to my lap, holding her to me as I deepened the kiss. Her body molded against mine. Every thick curve had me wanting to grip her tighter.

A soft whimper in her throat made me rock hard. The friction of her ass pressed against my throbbing cock was sinfully pleasurable. I wanted to bury myself inside her until she begged me to make her come.

She pulled back, putting her hands on my chest. "Jax."

Her phone rang, breaking the moment. She looked at the screen. "I'm sorry. I have to get this, or he'll assume I've been kidnapped and held against my will."

It must be her friend I met at the wedding. I spun her around so she still sat on my lap, but now her back was to me so I could hold her close. "But what if I did hold you against your will? If I remember correctly, that's what Beast does with his Beauty."

She giggled and swiped to answer the call. "Hey." She tensed and sat up straighter. "Oh no. Okay. Shit."

I leaned close to her ear to whisper. "Is everything okay?"

She only shook her head. "If I leave now, maybe I can fix it."

She hung up and pushed from my arms to stand up. "I'm really sorry, but I have to go back to work."

"What's wrong?"

"Nothing. I just have to go." She started walking.

I got up and ran after her. "Bryer, wait."

"Jax, this was really nice, but I..." She looked away, staring at the river.

"You what?" I wanted to know her secrets.

"I'm sorry."

I tipped her chin so she had to look at me. "Don't do that. You haven't done anything to apologize for."

She folded her arms, wrapping them around her chest. "I came." Tears threatened to spill from her eyes.

Fuck. Whoever caused her to cry should be eaten alive by rats. It's not my favorite method of torture, but it's effective. My ability to be *creative* was one of the first things Jacob noticed about me before offering me a job. It wasn't often we had to resort to torture, but when we did... it was my specialty.

"You're sorry you came?" I wiped the first tear that fell. "I'm not."

She glanced up at me. "Can you please take me back?"

"I will do anything you ask, as long as it's not putting you in danger. I can't do that, so don't ever ask." I took her hand and walked with her to the truck. Ensuring she was safely tucked into the passenger seat, I took my place behind the wheel.

Taking her hand, I pulled it back to my lap. "I have to leave town tomorrow for work but should be back the next day. Maybe we can try this again?"

"Jax?"

I gave her my attention.

"Did you mean what you said? About the monsters... you'd kill them?"

"Yes."

"How sad is it that I can't tell you who they are because I'm worried they'd be mad at me?"

"Baby girl, you don't have to tell me. I'll find them. Hunting is something I'm very good at." And I was about to become the scariest monster of them all.

Chapter 9

Bryer

Shit. Shit. Shit.

I shouldn't have left. And now Alice was gonna get fired.

My stomach twisted as we drove back to the restaurant. Jax was silent. But so was I.

He was everything I should be afraid of, but I didn't think he was half the monster he thought he was. He helped people. He saved them. I didn't care if he murdered assholes or tortured them. They were doing much worse to innocent people. For so many years, I'd wished for a knight to save me... and while I couldn't ask him to do that for me, he was doing that for others. For the first time, I had hope that the world wasn't as ugly as I thought, and my heart slowly found the stitches to begin knitting back together.

The only problem was it was knitting itself to Jax. It was too soon for that. I couldn't let my heart get involved. But how could I stop it? How could I walk away from this man who made me feel this safe so quickly?

Jax parked the truck, and I reached for the door handle.

"Angel, what did I tell you about rule number one?"

I let go. Having someone do something for me that I could do myself was strange. I wasn't sure if I liked it. The horrible feeling of being in debt to him for something as small as opening a door didn't settle well with me.

My door opened, and Jax reached in, grabbing me at the waist under his coat to lift me out. His hands were like hot coals, scorching my skin through my clothes. The way he made me feel had me wishing his hands were doing more than just touching me.

Maybe I wasn't broken after all. I thought for years that I'd been ruined. That I would never be sexually attracted to a guy. Or actually like being kissed.

But I did.

Even now, I could still feel his lips against mine, and I wanted more. Screw the slow burn, I didn't want to wait for the fire to fizzle out. I wanted to feed it until it was an uncontrollable inferno. I prayed it consumed me until I couldn't remember reality and what was right or wrong. I'd been so careful for so many years that I wanted to let myself enjoy what was before me.

But I had to walk away. I was going to enter a lion's den and didn't need Jax seeing how pathetic and meek I truly was. My dream of finding the fairytale ending was just that... a dream.

Jax leaned in to kiss me. His mouth pressed gently on mine, guiding me, teaching me. The way his hands snaked up my back to hold me closer had me forgetting why we were there in the first place. His body wrapped around mine, shielding me from the world. It was easy to think he was right, and nothing could harm me while I was with him. I felt safe in his arms.

He broke away first and leaned back to look into my eyes. "Let me see your phone."

I hesitated before handing him the old phone with a spiderweb of cracks across the screen.

He swiped and tapped the screen. His phone dinged, and he grinned. "There is never a time when I don't want to hear from you." He gave me a quick kiss. "I'll be back the day after tomorrow."

I gripped my phone like it was a lifeline directly to him and nodded.

He gestured to the restaurant. "I'll wait until you're inside."

Walking away from him was hard. It felt a little like free-falling from the sky. He was my parachute, but I couldn't take him with me.

The cold metal of the pull handle on the door was enough to swallow me up if I let it. What would happen if I chose not to go inside? Would Alice lose her job? Would I? Would something worse be waiting for me at the end of Rick's wrath?

Just when I was beginning to think there was hope, it was doused by uncertainty.

I looked back at Jax, leaning up against his truck. His focus was only on me. Even in the dusk lighting and shadows from his hat, I made out the slight grin lifting a corner of his mouth. If I could carry this moment with me, maybe it would be enough to protect my fragile heart while the world crumbled around me.

Pushing the door open, I was greeted by the wafting scent of prime rib and a bustle of energy. Silversmith's was busy with the early dinner crowd. I couldn't see Alice and worried she'd left before I could fix it.

Stacy motioned me over. She was a bubbly girl still in high school who worked evenings. "Girl, am I glad to see you. It's busy! Liv called off, and something is going down with Alice. She's in the office with Rick right now."

"Thanks. I'll be out as soon as I can to help." I hurried toward the office.

My phone dinged before I opened the door.

Beast: I don't think I can wait until the day after tomorrow to hear your voice. Call me when you get home, so I know you made it ok.

I couldn't believe he put his name as Beast on my phone. But there was no way I was going to change it.

"What are you grinning about?" Dani was outside the office, his arms folded as he waited for me.

"It's nothing." I stuffed the phone in my back pocket and took a long, steadying breath. "What happened?"

He raked a hand through his disheveled hair. "I don't fucking know. I was dropping your car off and overheard Rick ranting about you, so I eavesdropped enough to know he's pissed that you were gone. Alice has balls though. She's been in there with him ever since I got here, refusing to leave until you got here." He eyed the office door. "What the fuck set him off this time?"

I shouldn't have left. It was stupid to do something so selfish. "He told me I had to work a double today, but I made plans, so Alice said she'd cover for me."

"He's a rat bastard thinking he can use you like a slave." Dani's jaw ticked. "That's what he does, Bry. I don't understand why you don't just leave."

The weight of what he said held me under the figurative water, drowning me in the darkness I knew so well. I was no better than a prisoner, unable to make my own decisions or live a life outside these walls. "You know why. I'm trying to find work elsewhere, but without a car that runs well enough to get me out of town and enough money to live on, there's not much I can do."

"That's bullshit, Bry. I'll take care of you. We can leave and never look back, just like we said when we were kids."

"Except we're not kids anymore." I tried smiling for him. "Besides, Alice said I can move in with her. See? Things are already looking up."

"We should've left a long time ago." His voice was quieter now.

I hated thinking I was holding him back from life. I touched his arm and looked up into his eyes. "You can always go without me. But I have one condition. You have to send me postcards. I love those."

The sadness in his eyes hit me right through the heart. "I can't leave you, Bryer."

There wasn't time to go down that road right now. Dani declared himself a bodyguard of sorts over me, and I knew he thought if something happened to me, it would be his fault if he left. We'd had the talk many times. I started toward the office door.

Dani grabbed my hand, preventing me from opening it. "I'll be outside if you need me."

"Thanks, but I'll be fine. Go ahead and go home. I'll text you later." I pushed the door open before he could respond.

"Look who decided to show up." While I'm sure Rick held a jovial tone for the sake of Alice, he sneered in my direction.

Shutting the door behind me, I blocked out whatever curses Dani mumbled with it.

Alice sat stiffly in a chair across from Rick. "I'm sorry, Bryer. I didn't mean to cut your date short."

Rick's head snapped in her direction so fast it was a wonder his neck didn't break. "Date?"

Alice nodded. "That's why I was covering for her. She never does anything for herself, and I really wanted her to have a good time. This is just some stupid misunderstanding."

His jaw clenched, and I braced myself for a tongue-lashing. Or worse.

Rick continuously clicked the pen in his hand as he stared at me. "It is not a misunderstanding. Bryer and I had an agreement. She knew what she was doing. But it appears my *daughter* ignored her obligations and failed to show up for her assigned shift." I hated how he talked as if I weren't even in the room. "It's times like this that I hate being her boss and parent. As a father, I want to sweep it under the rug and ask her how her *date* went. But as her boss, I can't let it go. That would be unfair to my other employees."

I stepped forward. "I had it covered. Alice—"

He held up his hand as if to quiet me. "Ah, yes, Alice went above and beyond to ensure you could foolishly disregard your job."

Alice glared at him from her seat. "Mr. Wardley, that's not true. She's the one that goes above and beyond here. One afternoon off isn't a big deal, especially because the shift was covered."

He gave her one of his award-winning fake smiles. "I know it's hard to see someone you think is your friend do this to you, but Bryer shoving her responsibilities onto her co-workers is not your fault. I appreciate you picking up the slack, but I promise you won't have to do it again." He looked pointedly at me. "Will she?"

"No, sir." I looked down, away from them. I wanted to be anywhere else but in that office. Jax was wrong. The only worth I had was on the ground, stomped on, and buried in mud.

Alice gripped the arm of her chair. "I would do it again for her, *any shift, any day*."

"Yes, I'm sure you would. But if I let you, I could never teach Bryer a valuable lesson in accountability. You wouldn't deprive me of that. Would you?"

"Are we talking about the same Bryer? Because I've never met anyone with more—"

"Alice," he cut her off. "I think we're done here for the night. You're getting a little too upset, and I wouldn't want you to say something you'd regret."

She stood up, her chest heaving as she glowered over the desk. "Regret? Like... oh, I don't know, I quit?"

"Exactly. See? I don't know why you're so upset. Is it normal for you to react so aggressively?"

Her hands clenched and unclenched. "Mr. Wardley, I am not a violent person, but I strongly support standing up for myself and my friends when I believe they are being mistreated."

"I see. Well, Bryer... maybe you can help your friend out. Am I mistreating you, or do you deserve the reprimand for not following through on your side of our arrangement?"

I tried to swallow the lump in my throat. Words evaded me. All I could do was shake my head in response and hope it was enough.

Alice huffed and marched out of the office, shaking her head.

Rick gave an amused grin as he watched her leave. He sat back in his chair and resumed clicking the pen. "I assume you changed your plans to ensure you're available to close tonight?"

Close? I was so tired I wasn't sure if I would cry or drop from exhaustion before the night was over. "Yes."

He slapped the pen on the desk with a triumphant grin. "Well, I'm glad that's settled. I'm exhausted and going home. I'll see *you* later." The words fell off his teeth like a snare. He stopped next to me, leaning in. "If you can shirk your job for some guy, that tells me and the rest of the world just how easy you are. I've always said you were a little slut. Teasing all the men."

He grabbed his jacket from the rack by the door and left, leaving me to deal with the rollercoaster of emotions.

My stomach rolled.

Slut.
Whore.
You'd do anything for a guy.
Disappointment.
You can't say no.
Do that... Touch this... Kiss here.

The memories flooded me until the office was gone, and suddenly, I was sixteen again, afraid to shower while anyone was home. Locks didn't work; someone always had a key.

But there were other things I could do to keep *the intruders* from wanting sex. I mean... they still wanted it, but I refused to be what everyone thought I was.

You were always a little slut.

The office door swung back open, jolting me back into the present, and I stiffened until I saw Alice.

She marched over to me. "Why didn't you say anything? You just let him walk all over you." She pointed to the hall where Rick left. "I *knew* he was an ass. I could smell it a mile away, but this..." She closed her mouth and did a little jig with a scream. "This is ridiculous. He can't talk to you like that. Who does he think he is?"

"It doesn't matter. I need to go help Stacy. She was swamped when I came in." If I didn't stay busy, I'd end up crying.

Alice grabbed my arm and pulled me out of the office and back door. "She has three other servers to help. Make them earn their paychecks. You and I are gonna talk."

The sun had set, leaving behind shadows and illuminated street lamps. It was only five o'clock, but the high desert nights in late fall were cold, and I was grateful I never took Jax's coat off. I wrapped it tighter around me and followed Alice to her car. It was almost like having him with me, wrapping his arms around me. Protecting me...

Now I was just thinking silly. Neither Jax nor his coat could protect me. And if he could, why would he?

Alice started the engine and turned the heater on high. "I have questions."

I tensed. I wasn't sure I'd have answers. And my anxiety over Rick finding out I was skipping work again was killing me.

"First question." Alice placed her hands over the vents to warm them up. "Has he always been like this with you?"

If I told her the truth, would she believe me? Would he find out I said something negative about him? Oh, God, I didn't think I could handle this conversation.

She exhaled loudly. "Bryer, I want to help you, but I need to know the truth."

"Yes. But you can't tell him I said anything." Just openly admitting it scared me. That should be a red flag.

Her gaze narrowed. "Has he hurt you?"

My stomach lurched into my throat, and I had to redirect before I spiraled into a full-blown panic. "Ask me about the sex god."

"Bryer..."

"I can't. Please don't make me. You don't understand." Tears fell freely despite me willing them back.

"You know you can leave. You're an adult. You have choices." She grabbed her phone and started texting frantically. "I'll have my brothers meet us there in fifteen. They're big guys who can get you packed and loaded within the hour. Trust me, I've seen them do it."

I shook my head and placed my hand over her screen. "Please don't do that."

She dropped the phone to her lap. "Give me one good reason why I shouldn't?"

I couldn't. There wasn't one. But my mom would freak out if a couple of guys came to my apartment and started packing my stuff. I had to handle this delicately.

"It sounds much worse than it is. He's not a bad guy."

She folded her arms across her chest and stared at me pointedly. "That's what someone who's being abused would say."

"No." I shook my head. I needed to back-peddle out of this before she and everyone else looked at Rick differently. He'd be so pissed if anyone thought he was anything but the friendly, community-supporting, little league coach, good ol' guy who owned the town's favorite mom-and-pop restaurant. "It's really not that bad. Besides, I shouldn't have skipped my shift, then he wouldn't be so mad. It's my fault, really."

"Agh! Do you hear yourself?" She let loose a slur of curses. "You're moving in with me *tonight*."

"Alice, no." This was getting out of hand.

She let out an exasperated sigh. "I don't get it. If Rick is as big of an ass as I think, why not just move somewhere else?"

Because I knew Rick's deep, dark secrets he wanted to keep hidden from the world. He and my mom had plenty of those. "Seriously, can we talk about something else?"

"Fine." She sighed. "I suck at housekeeping."

"What?"

She shrugged. "If you're moving in, you should be warned."

I laughed. "Well, lucky for you, I don't." Cleaning was engraved into my DNA. My mom saw invisible dust and made me clean repeatedly. It was never clean enough for her, but she wouldn't get up and do any of the cleaning herself.

"Ah, the perfect roommate!"

"Can I take a few days to let things smooth over first?" I knew I was *allowed* to move. There wasn't a law I was breaking. I was of age. I wasn't mentally unable to care for myself or make decisions. I didn't need a conservatorship or any other type of guardian.

So why was it so hard? Why couldn't I just break free and live my own life? Why was I so scared?

"Bryer, I'm not trying to force you into anything, but…" Her brow knit together. "I'm not a therapist or doctor, but I know how Rick treated you tonight was wrong. There is no way I can just stand back and not say something."

"I appreciate you, I do. I'm just not ready. I have this irrational fear. It doesn't make sense, I know." I twisted my hands in my lap.

"I read something once that talked about narcissistic parents. I think this might fall in that category." Alice sighed, slumping back into her seat.

I chuckled to lighten the mood. "I don't know. I thought you said you weren't a therapist? That sounds an awful lot like a diagnosis."

She rolled her eyes and twisted in the driver's seat to face me. "Hear me out. It said that it's like that one thing people get when they're kidnapped and fall in love…"

Okay, now I laughed because this was not where I thought she was going. "Stockholm Syndrome?"

She snapped her fingers. "That's the one. Anyway, the article went on to say that adult children are trauma-bonded to the parent. It's like an addiction."

"So you're saying I'm addicted to Rick? Yeah, I promise you, I'm not." Just the thought made me want to laugh harder… or vomit.

She shook her head. "No. Well… yes. Shit, what did it say?" She chewed on her lip as she tried to remember. "There was something about a cycle when a parent gives their kid praise or something after their emotionally abusive outburst that can be addictive. It's called a trauma bond. Look, I'll find the article and text it to you to read for yourself."

It was my turn to roll my eyes. "You do that." I snuggled into Jax's coat and let his scent engulf me. I wasn't sure if whatever Alice said was true or not, but it kind of made sense. Not that I was ready to admit that to her.

She smiled coyly. "Now, how was your date with the sex god?"

While I was grateful for the subject change, I couldn't help the blush warming my cheeks. "It was short, but..." I grinned into the coat's collar. "He kissed me."

"Shut. Up." She shimmied in her seat. "Okay, tell me more. Was it like a peck on the cheek? On the lips? Some tongue action? Do NOT hold out on me."

I told her about the short date and kiss with Jax but left out all the murder and torture stuff. The more I thought about it, the more I was concerned there *was* something wrong with me. I had completely accepted Jax and his red flags without any rational logic. There were questions I still wanted to ask, but I believed his actions were valid, considering the circumstances behind them.

Maybe Alice was right, and I was addicted to danger or immoral actions. But if I was an addict, and Jax was my drug, I didn't want to be sober.

Chapter 10

Bryer

If I thought I was dead on my feet earlier, I clearly underestimated how much I'd feel like a truck ran me over by the time closing came around.

I couldn't even remember driving home. How I didn't wreck was beyond me.

All I could think about was plucking my contacts out and plopping onto my bed. Anything and everything else would have to wait until after I slept. I didn't work until one tomorrow and would probably sleep until then.

Trudging up the stairs, I had to will my legs to move with each step. A light was on in my apartment, but I was so groggy I didn't process what that meant until I opened my door and saw Rick and my mom waiting for me.

Fuck my life.

I hated that they had a key. Could nothing be private?

"We need to talk." Mom wrinkled her nose at me, probably assessing how badly I looked. I knew I was a hot mess. But running on two hours of sleep and enough caffeine to kill an elephant, I decided I didn't care.

I grinned. Someone else said those words to me before, and I couldn't help but think that was a lifetime ago.

I've already decided I don't care.

Jax didn't care that I was practically half his age. It didn't faze me either. Age shouldn't be a deciding factor between hearts.

Oh shit, there I was, letting my heart get involved again.

"What is so damn funny?" Rick barked.

I hadn't been paying attention in my sleepy delirium. "I'm just tired. What do you want to talk about?"

74

"It's obvious you don't care about us anymore. You went off with some guy and probably told him God only knows what kind of lies about us. You always were so dramatic." My mom stood up and began pacing. "What should we do, Rick?"

He ignored her and observed me. "Nice coat."

I kept my mouth shut.

He got up and strode toward me. "I think you need to remember we are your parents. No one else will ever love you the way we do. I took you in and raised you as my own when your real father didn't even want you."

Even after hearing those words on repeat for years, it didn't deaden the impact.

Mom stopped pacing long enough to splay a hand across her chest dramatically and stare at me with wide eyes. "Do you want to cut us out of your life? After everything we've done for you?"

"This is ridiculous! I never said that." I hated it when they twisted words around.

She marched closer, pointing a finger until it pressed to my shoulder. "You did when you decided to go behind our backs and tell lies about us."

"I haven't said anything. I promise." Well, technically, that was a lie. I did say something to Alice, but it wasn't much.

"Who does the coat belong to?" Rick crossed his arms and watched me, probably calculating what to say next.

"A friend." I tried to walk past them, but Rick stopped me.

"More secrets. Well, I have one for you too." He leaned in so close his breath was hot on my ear. "Since you like to spread your legs for just anyone, you might want to get paid for it."

I froze. I sincerely hoped he wasn't suggesting what I thought he was.

"I know you like to think I'm a slut, but I'm not." Tears fell down my cheeks, and I hated them. They showed my weakness, and they would use it against me. I just knew it.

"You can say you're not all you want, but it doesn't change the facts." Rick laughed and plucked at the sleeve of Jax's coat. "If you thought someone could truly like you, you're wrong. They know you put out and are only looking for a good time. There's nothing more to like about you. We've tried to tell you. We wanted to help you. But you just aren't that pretty and look at this body. Do you even care?"

It was verbal whiplash. My mind spun and tried to grasp just one thing to hang onto.

There's nothing to like about you.

Of course, that's what my mind caught hold of.

"As for earlier, I'm sorry I had to reprimand you in front of a co-worker. I can only imagine how embarrassing that would be. I really hope you don't put me in that predicament again."

"I don't understand what the big deal was. The shift was covered."

He took a step forward, making me take a step back. We did that until I ran into the door.

Reaching around me, he opened the door and pushed me outside. "The big deal is you didn't do your job. You ignored me and went against everything I said. I don't like it when people ignore me. I gave you a roof over your head. A job. I've been a father figure in your life. All for you to shit all over me. That's what the big deal is."

"Rick, I didn't mean to make you mad. I'm sorry." I stepped back, my foot on the edge of the first step.

"You should be sorry." He stepped once.

I grabbed the railing as tight as I could and leaned back, trying to keep as much space between us as possible.

"I won't let your horrible attitude ruin my night anymore. Get out of my way." He shoved me hard, and I lost my balance.

My grip faltered as I fell backward. The momentum of the fall carried me down each step until I landed on the ground. Pain shot through me. I gasped as I tried to catch my breath, but the wind was stolen from my lungs.

"Oh, shit!" Rick rushed down the stairs after me. "Bryer! Are you okay?" He squatted next to me. "You should have just moved out of my way, and this wouldn't have happened. Why would you do this?" He touched my leg, and not only did it send sharp pains up to my hip, but my stomach revolted against his touch.

"Don't touch me."

He removed his hands and raised them in surrender. "You are so stubborn. You knew I wanted to leave. You should have just moved."

My mom finally joined us. Not too fast for seeing her only child get pushed down a flight of stairs. "Oh, honey, are you okay?"

I was writhing on the ground, but yeah, ask the obvious.

Mom touched Rick's shoulder. "You should carry her into the house. There's no way she should be on those stairs right now."

"No!" I practically screamed. I was never staying another night in their house. It was the one promise I made myself when I turned eighteen that I've kept. I stumbled for more words. Anything to keep them from moving me. "I forgot Alice was picking me up tonight. I'm staying with her."

Rick glowered. "After a fall like this, you shouldn't be off visiting friends. You can't even get up."

"I'm fine. Just knocked the wind out of me." Okay, I was sure it did much more than that, but I needed them to leave me alone. Despite being in the worst pain ever, I forced myself to sit. "See? I'm fine."

I wheezed with each breath and wasn't sure I could stand yet, so I closed my eyes and focused on breathing.

"Maybe she needs a doctor?" My mom's voice rattled my nerves.

"No, she'll be fine. Besides, they ask a lot of questions at the hospital. They might mistake this as something it's not." Rick touched my shoulder.

I cringed but couldn't lean away.

"You really did it this time." His breath warmed my cheek as he picked me up.

No. No, no, no, no. Please. Anyone. Help.

"Put me down." Even as I said the words, I knew I couldn't walk on my own yet.

Surprisingly, he set me down. I gripped the stair railing and let out a cry. Tears trickled down my face. I took in an assessment of where I was the most injured. My feet felt fine, and my ankles were good. My right leg ached more than the left, but my hips were definitely bruised. I had a few cuts and scrapes, and my hand looked worse than it felt. By morning, I would probably look like I'd been beaten up and then run over by a semi-truck. Higher up, I didn't think I had any broken ribs, but maybe one out of place. It hurt to breathe. I was lucky I didn't break my neck. My arms were shaky, but to be fair, my entire body was trembling. It was probably shock.

I took the first step up, making sure to go slow. My legs were supporting my weight, but it was going to be a painful journey to my apartment.

"Bryer," Rick's voice lowered. "You shouldn't make me so mad." He clenched his fist. "If you wouldn't act out, I wouldn't get angry, and things like this wouldn't happen."

I was tired of saying sorry. It felt like it wasn't enough anyway, so why bother. I just nodded and took another step. I didn't even bother trying to hide the tears.

Once I reached my apartment, I shut the door and slid down it, curling up on the floor. Everything hurt. Wounds on the outside would heal, but my heart was past healing. Maybe it wasn't worth trying anymore.

The darkness that followed me wrapped its ebony fingers around my soul and squeezed. A sob racked through me, tightening the muscles around the already throbbing ribs. I wanted to scream and cry until there was no air left in me, but I couldn't. No sound escaped my throat.

I needed it to come out. I *had* to get it out. There was too much inside me, clawing its way through my skin.

Gasping for air, I reached for my phone. The screen was entirely shattered now. A new set of tears fell as I realized I couldn't even reach out for help.

But asking for help would mean I'd have to explain things. I would have to reveal the harsh truth I've kept hidden for so long.

I threw the phone across the room. It smashed into the wall and broke into pieces.

When I didn't text Dani, he'd come looking. But what would happen if I didn't call Jax? Would he think I didn't like him? That I was ghosting him?

As much as I wanted my bed earlier, I needed to soak in a hot bath more.

After I cried all I could, I picked myself up off the floor and headed to the tiny bathroom. I wasn't as shaky as before and could move a little better, but I was still surprised I hadn't broken anything. If there had been more steps, I might have.

The steam from the hot water filled the room. Undressing, I looked in the mirror and cringed. I already had bruises forming along my hips and sides.

I gripped the side of the sink, and a smear of red pooled under my palm. The cut on the side of my hand wasn't deep enough for stitches, but it would suck for a day or two. I looked up and wiped at the small cut above my eyebrow. I was sure it would look worse tomorrow.

Stepping into the bath, I bit down on my tongue to keep from crying out. Sitting took a bit of work, but it was worth it. I leaned my head back and wiped another tear away. I couldn't believe I fell down the stairs.

Well... *pushed* down the stairs.

The day had started with such a promise too.

I let the day's events unfold in my mind. Leaving with Jax had been scary, but I'd never felt safer. More alive.

He had been honest and open about who he was. It spoke volumes of how crazy I must be to be okay with it all. I wasn't scared. Not even a little. He told me he killed people for a living, and I didn't bat an eye. Most women in my situation ended up on the news, found in the dump, or stuffed in luggage along an old highway. But he was nothing but a gentleman with me.

And that kiss!

My fingers traced my lips as I thought about the kiss with Jax. Closing my eyes, I imagined his mouth on mine.

I may have been inexperienced, but he was not. The way his lips caressed mine aroused me. Every part of me tingled and warmed under his touch. When he placed me on his lap, I could feel the length of his hard cock pulsing at my center.

It had been seven years since the first and only time I'd had sex, but right then, I felt like a virgin. There was an intense throbbing between my legs—and it wasn't from falling down the stairs.

Slowly, I let my fingers glide from my lips to my collarbone. Like a feather, I grazed over my breasts. I sucked in a breath as the nipples peaked, begging for attention. Despite the pain I was in, this was what I needed.

Jax's face was all I saw as I pretended it was his fingers touching me. His voice guided me, telling me what to do—what he wanted to watch me do.

"*Go lower, baby girl.*" His voice guided me.

I hadn't ever played with myself before. Sex or any kind of foreplay hadn't been something that appealed to me. Not even self-play. After being subject to being the one to give pleasure, it always made me feel dirty. But with Jax... I *wanted* him to touch me. To do those things that I refused to let anyone else do to me.

I went lower, imagining what Jax might do. Spreading my legs slightly hurt with the tub walls hitting every new bruise, but I was beyond caring. Touching my clit, I let out a small whimper. I wasn't sure how or what to do from here.

Seven years ago, my ex-boyfriend tried to play with me, but it was awkward, and he did more fumbling around than anything. I gave up and just let him have sex. Once. It hurt more than anyone ever said it would, and I got nothing more out of it.

I wondered if Jax would fumble or know what he was doing. I highly doubted he was incapable. Even his kiss was experienced. It was that kiss that had me exploring right now.

I rubbed myself, finding a stroke that felt like I'd shatter if I stopped. Oh, God. Why haven't I done this before?

I spread my legs as wide as I could and dipped lower, pressing at my entrance. I hesitated, wondering if I should stop. But Jax's mouth was on me, kissing me, urging me to do more. Slipping a finger inside, I moaned.

"Jax." Saying his name while fingering myself felt right. He was the only one to make me feel this way. The only one I'd want to do this with. It was a shame he wasn't here for our *first time*.

My palm hit my clit as I thrust my finger in and out. With each slap, I went harder, loving the roughness. Fuck.

My stomach tightened, and I felt like I would explode. Was this it? Would I finally find a release that I desperately needed? Never having an orgasm before, I wasn't sure how to know if I'd reached that point. Whatever I felt right now was heavenly, and I could die happy with only experiencing that. But it wasn't enough. There was more hiding behind that pressure. There was an entire feeling I'd never known existed, and I craved it.

I cried out as I neared the precipice. "Jax." I wasn't sure if I'd screamed his name or whispered it. Reality was so far gone I only knew he was the one I wanted to go with me.

"Bryer?"

My brain was fuzzy, but I heard my name.

"Bryer!"

Oh no. Dani.

I pulled my hand away and was devastated to know I'd lost whatever was building inside me.

The bathroom door flung open. "Bryer?"

"Shit! Dani, get out!" I grabbed the towel close to the tub and pulled it down over me, soaking it thoroughly.

"Oh, fuck. I'm sorry." He placed a hand up over his eyes but didn't budge. "You didn't text or answer my calls. When I got here, your door was unlocked, and your phone was in pieces on the floor. And then I heard you yelling some guy's name." His face reddened. "Oh, shit. Oh, God. I'm so sorry. I didn't think... I... Fuck."

"Just get out, and we can talk out there when I have clothes on." I don't know what he was so embarrassed about. It wasn't him who was caught getting off, moaning some guy's name.

Grabbing my clothes, it took a hot minute to get dressed. I was careful not to rush it because my hips protested the idea of wearing sweats. But they were the softest, most comfortable article of clothing I could think of wearing after nearly killing myself. The oversized sweatshirt hid the rest of my bruises and prevented anything too tight along my ribs.

It still hurt to inhale, but not nearly as bad. I hoped a little rest would be just what the doctor ordered.

Dani paced outside the bathroom. "What the hell, Bry? What's going on?"

I inched my way over to my bed and sat down. Having a studio apartment had pros and cons, but right now, having easy access to my bed with company was definitely on the pros list.

"What the hell happened to you?" Dani sat next to me, and I winced when the mattress moved. "Fuck. Bry, are you okay? Tell me what's going on."

"I fell."

He raised a brow. "You *fell*."

"Sorry I couldn't text you. The phone kind of fell with me, and well..." I gestured to the broken pieces scattered on the floor. "It didn't survive."

He pinched the bridge of his nose. "*How* did you fall?"

"It was an accident. Rick and my mom were here, and I didn't move fast enough, and I fell."

"Son of a bitch. Bryer, you better tell me the truth. Did Rick hit you? Did he push you?"

"A little. But it wasn't his fault I fell down the stairs."

"You fell down the fucking stairs?" He stood up and looked down at me with wide eyes. "Did you break anything?"

I shook my head. "I don't think so. I'm actually feeling a lot better already. Just some bruises."

He scoffed. "You don't think? Fuck. Bry. I'm trying hard not to lose my cool here, but what the actual hell? You need to go to the hospital."

"I'm fine, Dani. Really. I just want to sleep and forget all about it."

"Well, that ain't gonna happen here." He spun and grabbed my suitcase from the top of my makeshift closet.

"What are you doing?"

"What does it look like? I'm getting you the fuck out of here. That's it. I can't do this anymore, Bry. You're leaving. I can't watch the abuse any longer. I know what they've done to you. I've been there for you after every time. I will always be there. But I can't watch you die." He pulled a dresser drawer open, grabbed undergarments, and stuffed them in the luggage. "Don't ask me to do that, Bryer."

"I'm scared." It was hard to admit that to anyone, but mostly him. He'd been my rock for so long that I worried if I told him I was afraid, he'd think it was because he wasn't doing enough.

He stopped to look at me. "I know you are. But so am I. I've been scared for years for you."

He returned to shoving clothes in the suitcase haphazardly.

"Dani, can I at least make one decision tonight?"

"Depends." He picked up one of my cutest tops and shook his head. "I will never understand your obsession with the color black."

I shrugged. My shoulders ached, but I tried to ignore the pain. "It's slimming. God knows I can use all the help in that department. Thick thighs and curves are the opposite of attractive."

"Shut up. I hate when you talk about yourself like that. You're gorgeous. There are a fuck-ton of guys out there who would love to die by suffocation by *thick thighs*."

I rolled my eyes. "I highly doubt that." I picked at a stray strand coming off the blanket. "But since we're on this topic. I have a question."

"Bry, if you ask me to fuck you, I'm duck-taping your legs together. The answer is no."

"Ew, gross. No." I cringed at the sour taste that filled my mouth at the thought of Dani being intimate with me. "I was just curious if you knew about toys and which ones might be good to get a girl to… you know… to come."

"Oh, shit. Ew. Damn. Now every toy is ruined for my future wife because I won't be able to scrub this conversation from my mind." He shoved some jeans in with the shirts. "I am the wrong friend to ask. Maybe ask Alice or another one of your girlfriends. But not me. Don't ever ask me again."

"Well, you already walked in on me—"

"Bry, so help me, if you don't stop talking…" He shook his head. "I can't unhear or unsee that. You know that, right?"

"Don't tell me you've never done that."

"I am not having this talk with you." He zipped the suitcase. "You're like my sister. I can't be picturing you doing anything that's not innocent."

"You know I'm not innocent." I hung my head, not wanting to talk anymore.

He tipped my head up. "You're more innocent than you realize." He helped me up. "Come on."

"Wait. You said I can make one decision tonight."

"I said it depends."

"I want to stay with Alice. I love you, but I think having another girl around will be just what I need."

"You can call her from the car. Right now, we are leaving."

We made it to the door before I froze. I didn't want to go down the stairs. I barely made it up them.

"I can carry you down." Dani set the suitcase down and picked me up.

I bit my tongue to keep from crying out. I didn't want him to feel bad for my pain. It wasn't his fault. He set me down by his car and went back for the luggage.

"Wait. Can you go grab my glasses and contacts?" I would be doomed without them. Well, not doomed, but it would suck.

Dani jogged back upstairs and came down with the last of my contacts and glasses. I got in the passenger side of his car and shut the door.

Was it only that afternoon I was reprimanded by Jax for opening my own door?

Rule one: I always open your doors.

Why?

To give me time to ensure the area is safe enough for my queen to enter.

Leaning my head back, I closed my eyes. For a moment, I was safe. I held onto that feeling and let myself drift.

Chapter 11

Jax

The clock over Jacob's desk in the office moved as slow as my watch. It was close to ten o'clock, and Diesel and I were going over everything before I headed out in the morning.

"The time is the same as it was three seconds ago." Diesel handed me the reports for Ana's Place.

Grabbing the manilla folder, I scoffed. "What's that supposed to mean?"

"It means I've been watching you check your watch every few seconds." He chuckled. "And we both know it isn't because you're excited about a new piece of jewelry."

"Fuck." I ran a hand down my face. "I need to distract myself."

After dropping Bryer off at Silversmith's, I couldn't focus on anything but that kiss. Whatever was going on between us was intense. We barely knew each other, but when I kissed her, there wasn't a part of me that didn't awaken. Her lips were like magnets drawing me in. I wanted to ravage them until they were swollen, and the only sound that could escape them was my name.

Bryer was the closest thing to an obsession I'd ever experienced.

"I'd say you already found one." Diesel slugged my shoulder and walked around the desk to sit.

He checked the computer once more before shutting it down. Bear was still in Michigan getting Ms. Albrecht ready to fly to Idaho, and his tracker hadn't moved from Callie's safehouse in over an hour. He planned to stay there overnight and leave tomorrow evening.

Diesel wasn't wrong. Bryer was a distraction, but in all the good ways.

He stood and gestured toward the door. "Well, I'm ready to go find my own distraction. If I'm lucky, she's already in bed."

"Sam shouldn't let you be so lazy."

"Lazy? Shit," he scoffed. "That woman makes sure I have my cardio in every night."

Immediately, I thought of Bryer. I wasn't sure if I could be so mundane with her. My heart raced, thinking of all the ways I could excite her. I would only want her *waiting in bed* if I told her to be there. If I had a plan to draw out the night and give her instructions to stretch out the anticipation.

My cock twitched, thinking of her naked and spread out, waiting for me. Her fingers teasing her clit but never coming. I wanted to be the only one to make her come. If she had to do it herself, I failed as her man.

Her man.

Shit. Two days later, I was utterly and irrevocably addicted.

"I'm staying in the guest room tonight. If Flapjack finds *his* distraction tonight, I won't sleep." We both laughed, and I followed him out of the office. "Besides, I need to leave by three to get to the airport on time."

"It will be nice when the other houses are ready. Jacob said they're breaking ground for three next month. I think he's got plans for three more not long after that. We'll have a fucking suburb up here."

Living in Northeastern Nevada, the land was still wild and unclaimed. Most of it still had never had a footstep taken on it. Jacob could build an entire city up here on the mountain for all I cared. Being an hour away from town meant peace and quiet, but the ranch was a front for our real business. If everyone believed we were all ranchhands, the less they asked questions. "I, for one, will be happy to not share walls with the fucking mafia daughter and her husband."

Diesel laughed. "It can't be that bad."

"I'm all for being creative, but there are some things a brother should never hear."

Diesel's laughter deepened, and he shook his head, clamping a hand onto my shoulder. "I'll see you when you get back."

He left, leaving me in the blissfully quiet main house. It wasn't often I stayed in here. I could count on one hand how many times I'd done it on purpose.

I grabbed my bag filled with clothes earlier. It was on the end of the guest bed across from the office. With six bedrooms and three bathrooms, the main house was large enough to fit all three bunkhouses and still had room to spare. Well, they weren't technically bunkhouses but doublewide manufactured homes.

And one day soon, I'd have one to bring Bryer home to.

Taking my hat off, I smirked, tossing it on the bed. I couldn't believe I was thinking of bringing her *home*.

Please don't let this be some sick joke. It would destroy any ounce of humanity I had left if my angel wasn't real. If God could give a devil an angel to love, that very devil would protect her from the demons that consumed his world because she would hold his soul.

Bryer might not be mine to claim, but it was too late. She already held my heart. I would confess every sin I'd ever done on my knees while worshipping her. There wasn't any of her monsters who could hide from me. I would hunt them all and make them beg for her forgiveness. But they would never hear it. My angel would be far from the pits of hell.

My cock throbbed, begging for a release, but nothing could quench the fiery desire burning her name onto my soul until I was buried deep inside her. Even then, I don't think I would be satiated.

After checking my watch again, I grabbed my sweats from my bag. Maybe a cold shower would help.

The bathroom was almost as big as my room. River rock lined the shower walls and floor, surrounded by glass. Adjusting the water, I stepped in.

Fuck that was cold.

My hard-on didn't leave. The strain from restricting any pleasure ached with each pulse.

Grabbing my cock, I almost groaned. Bracing an arm on the wall, I leaned into my hand.

Getting myself off wasn't new. I hadn't been with a woman in a long time. I had a few flings, but nothing long-term. But with Bryer... that's all I wanted. A lifetime of watching her smile, hearing her laugh, making her come over and over as she writhed on our bed...

My hand moved with each thought, getting dirtier and dirtier. Sliding over my thick erection, I imagined Bryer on her knees, taking me into her mouth until she couldn't breathe. Filling her until she gasped for air and sucked me down until I came.

I could chase her through the woods, stalking her until she was so wet I could smell her... hunt her.

Fuck.

I pumped faster, fisting myself tighter. Her pussy would be begging for me, weeping with her sweetness that I would drink up as she rode my face.

I released, shooting the wall in a steady stream. I leaned my head back and moaned her name.

My perfect angel would be mine. And she would give me her innocence. I would be her beast.

The plane touched down in Texas. I checked my phone for the hundredth time since waking, but there were still no missed calls or texts.

I gave Bryer time, but now I was getting worried. Had I moved too fast? Kissing her felt so natural. She reacted the way I'd hoped and seemed to enjoy it as much as I had.

I twirled a toothpick over my tongue before clenching it between my teeth. Was she okay?

Fuck. I couldn't start thinking she was hurt or worse because she wasn't calling. But knowing what I knew and the job I had, I knew better than anyone how one missed phone call could mean the difference between finding them in time and something much uglier.

Fuck it. I pulled my phone back out and opened up the texts.

Beauty.

I grinned, thinking of how appropriate it was that my beauty loved that particular fairytale.

Me: How much begging do I need to do to get my angel to call me?

Nothing. Not even left on read. At least then I'd know she was reading them and only ignoring me. My gut twisted, and I had to remind myself not every damsel in distress is kidnapped. Maybe she forgot to charge her phone? She worked a double yesterday. She could still be sleeping. It was only seven o'clock back home.

A car was waiting to take me to Ana's Place. It wasn't a commercialized safehouse. Only those Jacob employed knew about it and, of course, those who lived there.

It took an hour to drive to the safe house, but there was no possible way to have something like this in the middle of a city.

Tressa was a sweet woman who had the world fall down around her when she was sixteen. She had met someone online who promised her love. She ran off to meet him, but it wasn't the guy she thought who met her. It was a predator who hid behind a screen.

Her parents hired Jacob, but she'd been gone almost a year by then. When we found her, she was broken, lost, and ashamed to return to the world. Jacob made sure her parents knew she was alive but offered her a place here that she accepted eagerly. That felt like forever ago. Now, she helped those we brought to the Place.

Tressa met me out front, welcoming me with a hug. "How was your flight?"

I heaved my bag over my shoulder and gave a short nod. "Not bad. How about you? How's life down here in the oven? Shit, it's almost November, you'd think it would cool down."

She shrugged. "One day it's eighty, and the next it will be thirty-two." Laughing, she closed the gate and entered the security code, locking it.

"Anyone who lives in Texas is made of something dark and twisted." I winked at her and walked with her to the main building.

It was more of a mini fifty-room resort than anything else. Jacob thought it would help to have everyone in one spot with their own rooms for privacy. There were also three offices, one for Jacob, me, and Tressa. A giant mutual space, dining room, therapy room, kitchen, a small movie theater, and an indoor/outdoor pool filled the rest of the place.

He had live-in housekeeping, cooks, and two therapists. Tressa oversaw everything. Her job was crucial in helping us keep everyone safe and things running smoothly.

"How is everyone doing?" I unlocked my office, which had a bedroom located off it, and dropped my bag near the door.

"Assuming you mean the last group from the island?" She sighed. "Acclimating."

"That doesn't sound good." I walked to my desk and pulled out my phone. Still nothing.

"It's not. I'm worried. They hide from each other like if they see another girl from the island, they *know* what happened to them. The youngest one was only twelve. She's been hiding in her room, not talking to any of the other girls here. And most of them are afraid of Benny, which makes it hard for him." She sat down in the chair across from me. "I don't want to have a separate home for boys, but maybe it would be best."

"We're already working on that. That's one of the things I wanted to talk to you about." I put the phone down, face up, so I wouldn't miss Bryer's call. Or text. Hell... I'd take morse code at this point.

Tressa sat up straighter. "I'm all ears."

I chuckled. "Well, Jacob sent me with a proposal." I got up, grabbed the files from my bag, and returned to the desk. "He's already started construction on it, and it should be done around spring next year. It seems we are outgrowing Ana's Place."

"Not all the rooms are full, but we're close."

I nodded. "That's why he wants to build on. Expand. Next summer, he wants to add an additional hundred rooms. This is what we need to talk about."

"A hundred rooms?" She slumped in the chair. "Wow. I hate saying this, but I'm gonna need help."

"That's what we thought. We want you to continue running Ana's, but you'll need at least one assistant manager. Would you like us to find one, or do you think there is someone here you trust to help?"

Tressa pressed a finger to her temple and rubbed. "Can I think about it?"

"Of course." I pushed a second envelope across the desk that was addressed to her.

She picked it up and opened it. "What's this?"

I held my hands up. "I'm only the messenger."

"Jax, that's a hundred thousand dollars." Her hands shook as she pulled out the check. "Addressed to me."

If she was stunned over that, she'd pass out seeing one of my checks. I stopped counting the zeros in my bank account years ago. I could only imagine Jacob's. He had his hand in a few honey pots. None of which were legal, I'm sure.

But then he gave back so freely. Like building mini resort safe houses for survivors.

I chuckled and sat back in my chair, threading my fingers together in a steeple. "Tressa, I do believe that's a bonus."

"A bonus is a hundred dollars... this is a year's pay!"

"Put it in savings. Go on a vacation. Buy yourself a new wardrobe. Hell, I don't care, and I know for damn sure Jacob doesn't care what you do with it. It's yours. You've earned it."

"I already put my paychecks in the bank. You don't charge rent. All the food I could want is provided. Even therapy is free." She stared at the check. "I have been thinking about visiting my parents, though."

"Oh?" This was news. Tressa hadn't left the safehouse since arriving.

"I've been talking to them on the phone more. I miss them." She lowered her eyes and dropped her hands to her lap, still holding the check.

I couldn't stop myself from eyeing the phone. What was taking Bryer so long to respond? "Have you talked to them about a visit?"

"I have. They're excited. It's been... too long." She straightened up. "But that's not why you're here. I suppose you want to have a look around? Check on the girls yourself?"

What I wanted was to fly back to Nevada, walk up to Bryer, and kiss her. Then ask her why the fuck she hasn't called. "Yeah." I stood and put the phone in my pocket. "After you," I said, gesturing to the door.

"So, tell me more about the other safehouse." She led me down to the main room.

The décor was modern, with just enough country to fit in Texas. Paintings littered the walls, and I realized half were from more than one of the girls who still stayed with us at Ana's.

I stopped to look at one. "I don't remember these."

The painting spoke to me, with gradient swirls of blacks and greys growing darker toward the edges. In the middle was a single red rose.

"They are incredible, aren't they?" Tressa folded her arms and looked at it with me. "Isabelle is the artist."

"Isabelle?" I smiled fondly as I recalled when I first saw her. She was one of the girls from Panama.

With no parents or relatives that she could remember, her best shot at life was to bring her here. From what we gathered, she had been in the trafficking ring since she was a small girl. We gathered enough information to know she had been taken around eight and was now almost sixteen. Not the youngest in that group, but maybe one of the longest to survive.

"Do you think she'd sell this one to me?" I turned and continued toward the mutual living area.

Tressa laughed. "For you? She'd probably give it away for free."

"How's she doing?" I worried about all the survivors, but some clung to my darkened heart more than others.

"Ask her yourself, she's over there." Tressa pointed to the corner where the small library sat, nestled away from the main foot area traffic.

Isabelle's long dark hair hung freely over her shoulders, complimenting her sun-kissed complexion. She was curled up on the oversized chair with a book. A smile slightly lifted the corners of her mouth.

I knocked on the open door. "Hey, stranger."

She looked up, wide eyes immediately locked on me. Her face softened, and she got up, rushing over. "Jax!" She hesitated, then reached out for a hug.

I never touched any of them without permission but happily embraced her back. I wanted them to know not all men were the evil scumbags they'd been forced to serve.

"What are you doing here?" She pulled back and set her book down.

"I came to check in with everyone. Make sure you're okay." I leaned against the doorframe and hitched a thumb over my shoulder. "That's some pretty impressive artwork."

She blushed. "Thank you. It's helping me cope. Art doesn't need me to be good. I can get out what I'm feeling with a paintbrush and paint."

"Would you be willing to sell me a piece?"

Her eyes lit up. "Really? You'd want one?"

I nodded. "The one with the rose in the middle."

"That one was hard to paint. I couldn't get it right. I had so much darkness consuming me." She sucked in a long breath.

"We have something in common," I whispered. It wasn't meant for her to hear.

"You can have it." She marched past me. I followed a few steps behind as she snatched it from the wall and handed it to me. "Here. It's yours."

"Thank you. But I *will* be paying you for it." I held the painting and couldn't help but think of Bryer. She was the rose, surrounded by demons.

Oh, but what a demon I would be for her.

My phone buzzed in my pocket, and I grabbed it. "Excuse me for a moment."

It wasn't my angel calling, but Diesel. "Hey."

"I see you landed and made it okay."

I snuck down a hallway to find a place to talk. "Is there really a reason to track me? Shit, you're like a kid with a new toy."

"Bear called. He said he still plans to leave tonight. He and Wes have a flight plan to leave Michigan at ten. Are you still coming back tomorrow?"

"That depends." I couldn't help the gut-wrenching feeling that something was wrong with Bryer. "Can you do me a favor?"

"You sound serious. What's going on?"

"I need you to check on someone for me. Her name is Bryer. She works at Silversmith's. I don't have a last name, but it will be Harper one day, so I don't have to tell you how important this is to me."

"Damn. You can't just spring that on me. I can't be expected to keep a secret like you're getting married from Sam. Or the guys."

"Diesel," I growled his name.

"Okay, okay. Is this the girl from the wedding?"

I looked down at the painting. "Yeah. I can't explain it, but she's it. She's the one."

"And you want me to check on her? Did you not get your future wife's number?"

I didn't have a toothpick and could feel the anxiety creeping in. "I have her number, but she's not answering."

"Is she in some kind of trouble?"

Fuck I hoped not. "Shit. If I knew, I wouldn't be asking you to help."

My heart began to race. Flickers of my past raced through my mind. I set the painting down and dug in my pockets, looking for a stray toothpick.

Breathe in. Breathe out.

"Jax?" Diesel called my name. "Hey, I wasn't trying to set off a trigger. You still there?"

"Yeah." I ran a hand through my hair and tried to focus on the painting. Bryer was fine. She wasn't *her*.

The woman in my dreams, haunting me, reminding me of why I had to leave my life—my family.

"Stay with me, Jax." Diesel's voice was far away as the memories flooded me.

It was a different time. A different life. A different country.

I was supposed to find her. The target. My mission.

Alison McDere' was an innocent journalist caught at the wrong place and time. Her pleas captured my attention as I watched the ransom video from the group of terrorists for the hundredth time.

But she wasn't just some girl. She was my sister's best friend. And her pleading was personal. She begged for me, Jack Granger, to save her.

I was commanded to lay low. She was only a journalist and wasn't worth invading an entire city to rescue. They were going to try, but there were no promises, and I had too much of an emotional connection, so they wouldn't let me go.

Bullshit. Right then, I decided the rules didn't apply to me. I went AWOL and left to find her myself. I knew they wouldn't get to her in time.

It took me a week, but I found Alison. I heard her cries before I saw her. I knew it was her, and I cursed under my breath.

When I snuck in, I didn't think. I just reacted.

I used a knife to keep quiet until I got close enough to the room where she was being held. A man was grunting like a pig as he raped her on the trash-littered floor. She was bloody and beaten to where she was nearly unrecognizable.

Her sad whimpers tore through me, and I went mad. I put a bullet in the man's skull and ripped him off her. She wouldn't look at me.

"Alison, it's me. It's Jack." I tried to smooth her hair from her face.

She screamed and panicked, rolling to get away from me. "Don't look at me. Don't touch me! Just kill me!"

I couldn't do that. I'd known Alison since she could walk. She was the girl who drove me nuts when she came over and stayed with my sister. She was like a sibling. I couldn't kill her. "I'm here to save you. It's me. You know me."

"No!" She shook her head and clawed at her skin. Blood streamed from the fingernail cuts. "NO!" Tears fell as she began to sob.

I stepped closer, crouching with her. "Alison."

"Get away from me!" She choked on the sob. "Don't look at me!"

"I'm not leaving you here." I shoved my gun in its holster at my hip and picked her up. "Stop screaming, or you'll kill us both."

There was no telling how many men were on their way. I jogged out of the room and made it to the stairs when I heard the gunshot and felt Alison's body jerk.

I flung her over to cover her and heard the gun drop to the floor with her hand. I reached for my gun, but it wasn't there. She'd taken it and shot herself.

I wiped her face, smearing blood and hair, and kissed her. "Why?" I asked her over and over, even though she couldn't answer.

I sat there with her for what felt like hours, cradling her on my lap. The sun had set, and footsteps echoed in the house. But I didn't care. I failed her.

"Sargeant Harper, you have to let her go. She's gone, sir."

I barely registered who was there or why. I was numb and felt myself drowning in the darkness. I looked up and recognized my second in command. They would have been too late to save her.

But it didn't matter. She was dead.

"She's going home." I got up, carrying her lifeless body with me. No one talked to me as we made our way to the base. I was court marshaled and held in lock-up, ready to be sent back to the US for my hearing. But at least Alison would be going with me.

Word of my actions made it to Jacob Cardosa. Apparently, he needed another man with my expertise in tracking and pulled a few strings. I didn't even know men like him existed.

But it wasn't before I had one last message sent to me via the group leader of who was the father of the man I killed. The one raping Alison.

We will kill everyone you love and make you watch.

Jacob and I decided if I was dead, there was no reason for them to retaliate. And so far... it worked. There hasn't ever been any sign of the bastards finding out I lied and was alive.

But my first thoughts went to Bryer. If they found out, did they get to her? Did they have her?

I couldn't breathe.

I dropped to my knees.

"Jax." It was Diesel.

I held the phone tightly in my hand. "You have to check on her."

"I am. Right now." There was some mumbling on his end of the line. "Flapjack is tracking her down, and we'll let you know as soon as we know anything. Don't worry. I'm sure she's okay."

I nodded even though he couldn't see me.

"Jax?" Isabelle found me, kneeling beside me. "Are you okay?"

I nodded again. "I'm fine. I just need..." A toothpick. But I couldn't say the words. I needed Bryer. I had to know she was okay. Fuck.

Did I do this to her? I was selfish in thinking I could have someone in my life.

"Jax." Tressa crouched with Isabelle. "What's going on?"

"I just need a minute."

They both nodded and left. One thing about being in the safe house was that everyone respected each other. Everyone dealt with their past and triggers differently.

"Shit." Diesel was back on the line. "Jax..."

"No." I shook my head. "No."

"She's not at home, but she's not scheduled to work until one. She could just be out shopping or some shit."

"Find her. I'm on my way." I grabbed the painting and found the girls in the central area. "I'm sorry, but I need to cut this visit short."

"Is everything okay?" Isabelle looked worried.

"Someone very special to me might need help."

"Then you have to go." Tressa folded her arms. "Is she... is she in danger?"

I clenched my jaw. God, I hoped not.

Chapter 12

Bryer

I yawned and stretched, regretting the movement immediately. Ouch. Holy shit. I'd forgotten I fell down a flight of stairs for a moment.

My ribs were severely bruised, but I think my hips were worse. I was in Alice's spare bedroom. It was strange how well I slept there. Usually, I couldn't sleep anywhere new. Especially someone else's house. It stemmed from my childhood and how untrusting I was with people. To be fair, most people showed me their true colors at an early age.

I could remember the first time it happened. I was seven, and my mom wanted to party at a friend's house. She loved that life and didn't want to stop. So, she brought me along, making me sleep on foreign couches or beds.

Every time, I pleaded with her to not take me. I tried to fight her, do whatever I could to keep her from making me go. But it was no use.

She would slap me across the face and yell at me. Then… she would tell me to go to bed. But it wasn't my bed. It was *his*.

It was dark in there. I couldn't see much with the light seeping in under the door. But each time we were there, he would be the one to *check on me*.

"Touch it." He instructed as he held his dick out for me, forcing my fingers to touch it. He held onto me, keeping my hand gripped around it the best my little hands could.

"Open your mouth. Shhhhh… Don't tell anyone. It's our secret game."

My stomach rolled with the memory, and I ran from the bed to the bathroom. I found the toilet and threw up.

Alice knocked on the door. "Bryer? Are you okay?"

I closed my eyes in shame. Tears ran down my face. "I'm fine."

"It doesn't sound fine."

I sniffed back the sobs. "I just think the shock wore off. I'll be out in a minute."

I rested my head on my arm, hanging over the toilet. "You're okay. You're okay." I repeated it until I stopped crying.

I'm safe. I exhaled slowly. *I'm safe.*

Taking Alice's mouthwash, I free-falled enough to rinse my mouth and returned to the guest room. Jax's coat was on the end of the bed. I picked it up and wrapped it around me. He was my security blanket. Or, at least, his coat was until I saw him again. *If...* I saw him again.

Sneaking out to the living room, I felt like a lost puppy. Looking around, I wasn't sure if there was a place I couldn't sit, so I stood. How had I never been to my friend's house before?

Oh, yeah... that's right. I didn't have a freaking life.

Alice was busy loading the dishwasher. "I told you I suck at housekeeping, but I didn't want your first day here to be overwhelming, so I've been trying to pick up. But," she shook a dirty water glass at me, "don't expect me to be like this every day. I wasn't kidding."

I smiled. "You don't have to do that. Honestly, that makes me feel more anxious than if you'd just leave it. And if you don't mind, I'll pick up when I'm ready. Cleaning helps me think and calm down. I swear it's not personal."

She tossed a plate on the bottom rack as if she'd never loaded the thing a day in her life. "Well, then, I'm totally leaving this until later." She shoved the rack in and closed the door.

I chuckled and looked around. It wasn't as bad as I thought it would be. "The guest room is nice. Thank you for letting me stay last night."

"Uh, no. That's your room. Remember? You're moving in with me, and after last night, I'm not taking no for an answer. My brothers are coming to help get the rest of your things this weekend. It will be like having a group of bodyguards doubling as movers. Just take the help and say thank you." She grabbed a bottle of water from the fridge and plopped down on a big lounge chair. She gestured to the kitchen. "There's not much, but it's all yours. I don't care about hoarding food. If I buy it and you want it, eat it. Except for the M&M's. Trust me. When our cycles sync up, those are gonna save us both." She winked and chugged her water.

I wasn't sure what to say. Thank you felt too weak, but I wasn't sure there was a stronger, more meaningful word. "We should talk about rent and utilities. I don't want to be mooching off you."

"It's not mooching, but sure, let's talk. My parents bought me this house, so it's paid for. I'm not worried about money if you haven't noticed." She tossed the empty water bottle, and it landed in the trash can. "Score!"

I laughed and started to feel a bit more relaxed.

"Are you going to stand there all day?"

"I guess I'm still getting used to being here. Where do I sit?"

"Anywhere." She swung her arms out wide.

I took the end of the big, fluffy, oversized couch and snuggled in. Oh, this was nice. I curled up my legs and wrapped the coat around me tighter. I could definitely get used to this.

"See? It's comfy as hell, isn't it." She clapped her hands. "Okay. So, how about we circle back to this conversation in three months, but to have a bit of security, let's just say rent won't be more than two hundred a month and half utilities?" She tapped her chin. "Oh, and guys are not allowed to move in with us without permission from either of us. But staying the night is definitely allowed." She wiggled her eyebrows. "About that... I think I want to take you up on that offer for you to give Dani my number."

Grinning, I held out my hand. "Give me your phone."

She eyed me curiously but gave it to me.

Thankfully, his number was one I knew by heart. I tapped his number in, saved it to her contacts, and then sent him a text.

Alice: It's Bryer. This is Alice's phone number. Don't be a dick. Call her.

I handed it back to her. "You're welcome."
The phone rang almost immediately.
She looked at the screen and buried her face in a throw pillow.
I got up and let her talk to Dani without me eavesdropping. There was only one guy I wanted to talk to, but I couldn't. His number was on a phone that no longer worked. Sighing, I went back to the room and looked around.
It felt weird, but this was now my room. I should start letting it soak in. But I just couldn't bring myself to unpack anything just yet. If I lived out of my suitcase for a week, that was my problem. It wouldn't hurt anyone else.
I shrugged off my sweats and shirt, leaving Jax's coat on the bed, and dressed. Well, I didn't need a mirror to see the bruises. The clothes I picked out were the softest I could find without being a pajama hog all day.
One thing I learned early on was to get ready every day. Even if I didn't feel like it. There was something about being finished to keep the depression from killing me.
Piling my hair up in a cute but practical messy bun, I felt more confident. I slipped a new pair of contacts onto my eyes and returned to where Alice was still on the phone with Dani.
She giggled and wiggled in her seat. Hanging up, she tossed her phone at me. "I can't believe you did that!"
I rolled my eyes and threw it back at her. "It looks like you're soooo mad about it."
"He asked me on a date."
"Yeah? Well, he'd be lucky to have you on his arm." It was too soon to say, but these two might be perfect for each other.
"He's not fake, right? Like, he's a good guy?"
"One of the best." For years, he'd been the only one I could trust. I sighed and curled back up on my spot on the

couch. "So, how pissed do you think Rick will be if I call off today?"

Alice scoffed, grasping at her chest. "Excuse me? Um, girlfriend, last night when you were pushed down a flight of stairs, was both of us quitting that fucking place."

"I can't. There's not a place around here that will hire me."

"Says who? Rick? He doesn't fucking own the entire town, and I can assure you, there are plenty of people out there who think he's an asshole too. You've just been looking at the wrong jobs."

I was scared to let her words create any hope. "I don't know."

She picked her phone up and dialed a number. Holding her finger up, she gave me the signal to hold on. "Hi. This is Alice. Can I speak with my dad?"

I leaned forward and listened. What was she up to?

Her face lit up. "Hi, Daddy!"

After a couple of yeses, nos, and one I promise... she cleared her throat. "I was actually calling because you remember my friend I told you about? Bryer? Well, she's now my roommate, and we're both looking for a new place to work."

There was a slight pause from Alice. "No. We both quit in solidarity. The owner is a jerk."

I tensed, thinking she was about to tell him what happened.

"Oh, it was for a very good reason! One I would like to tell you in person. It's serious. You know I wouldn't leave a job like that if it wasn't."

She gave another yes... no... yes. "Thank you, Daddy!"

After hanging up, I gave her one of the longest *what the heck* stares I could manage.

She grinned wider. "All I need is your resume."

"I don't have one."

"Then we make one, duh." She got up and left to her bedroom, returning with a laptop. "It's easy. And my dad said he knows of a few places that might be hiring a couple of girls like us, and he'd be happy to hand in our resumes personally."

I pushed my brows together. "I'm not sure how that will help."

"My dad is Arthur Walton. He owns Great Basin Nevada Electric Company."

"Your dad owns the power company?" Holy shit. No wonder she wasn't stressed about money. "That still doesn't explain how it can help me get a job."

"There are enough people who know him that when he does something like handing in a resume for someone, that person is hired on the spot. No interviews. No training. Just hired." She shrugged. "It's a perk. Love it and say thank you."

I laughed. "Thank you." Now, only if it worked.

Things were looking up. Maybe I could find a way to contact Jax and let him know I didn't ghost him.

"Hey, does that magic last name have a way of finding anyone?"

"Whatcha thinking?" She grabbed her phone and readied her fingers.

I laughed again. At this rate, my side was gonna hurt from being happy, not bruises. "Jax. I don't know his last name, but I was supposed to call him last night, but… well… my phone kinda shattered into a few pieces after my fall."

She gasped. "Girl! No." She got up and paced. "Okay, first we backtrack. He was at the wedding we catered. You said he was security?" She snapped her fingers. "Cardosa. Yeah. Let's look there first and see what we find."

Her fingers flew across her laptop keyboard as she googled Cardosa, Elko, Nevada.

Her eyes went wide when the search came back with articles of Jacob Cardosa and a ton of police reports. All of which made Jacob look like a hero.

"It says here that he owns a ranch about an hour north of Elko." She clicked again and again. "Bingo. Look. I found your sex god."

She turned the screen so I could see the image of Jax and Jacob. The picture was from about three years ago, but Jax looked exactly the same. Even in picture form, he made me feel hot and bothered.

Jax Harper.

At least now I had a last name to go off. "Can we find his number?"

"We can try." She clicked and typed like she was an undercover agent on a mission. "Shit. I can't get anything on him. Or Jacob. Or any of his guys. Their public image is just that." She looked at me. "I don't know who Cardosa is, but he only shows the public what he wants them to see. And my friend... their phone numbers aren't it."

I pouted, slumping into my seat. "That just sucks."

She twitched her lips as she thought. "We could drive out and maybe find the ranch?"

"And get lost on a dirt road where we eventually run out of gas and eaten by mountain lions? No, thank you."

"It's supposed to snow tonight anyway." She let out an aggravated groan. "I *hate* snow."

"I don't know. As long as I don't have to drive in it, snow is kinda peaceful." It absorbed the sound and hid the ground. As strange as it was, snow gave a sort of comfort. As long as nothing had touched it, it created a cocoon of protection. But if someone trudged through it, the magic was gone.

Just don't ask me to drive in it.

"I guess we could order some pizza and watch a movie? I'm a sucker for a Korean Romance."

Oh my gawl, my roommate was a K-drama fan. "As long as I don't cry. I can't do crying movies."

"So, you'll watch one with me?"

I sighed, giving in. "You have to promise I won't be crying at the end."

She held her pinky out. "Promise."

I couldn't believe I was doing this. I hooked my finger with hers. "Deal."

Chapter 13

Jax

The plane touched down, and I practically bolted from the cabin. Dialing Diesel, I jumped into my truck.

He answered on the second ring. "Hey, okay, so here's the thing. She didn't show up for work."

My mouth dried, and the toothpick tucked between my teeth snapped in two as I clenched my jaw. I spit it out, quickly grabbed another from the glove compartment, and focused on the present news. "So where is she?"

"I have an address, but no one has seen her all day. According to one of her co-workers, it's a little apartment over a garage."

I hit the steering wheel. Fuck! "Text me the address." I hung up and waited for his message to arrive, then typed it into my GPS for directions.

The sun was already setting. Damn, planes are fast, but it still took almost four hours. Not including drive time to the airport.

The short daytime hours made it feel like I had been gone longer than I was. But I now worried I might have been gone too long.

Hell, I couldn't stop myself from thinking if I just hadn't left...

I parked across the street from the address and stared at the apartment. No lights were on, and I saw no movement. Shutting the truck off, I scanned the area. The main house had a light on, and a shadow crossed in front of the window.

Could Bryer be in there?

I twirled the toothpick, letting it click over my teeth. Fuck this. I exited the truck and jogged over to the stairs leading to the apartment. Taking them two at a time, it didn't take me long to reach her door.

I knocked, waiting for her to open it and tell me I was freaking out for no reason. But I tensed when I didn't hear anything. Nothing. Not even a creak of a floorboard.

I tried the handle, and it opened. Stepping inside, I flipped on the light, and my heart dropped. The small studio apartment was in disarray. Not the typical mess of an unkempt house, but a hurried mess. Like whoever was here left fast.

I spotted the cell phone first. Squatting, I picked up the main piece. My stomach rolled. It was Bryer's. I recognized the model and the spiderwebbing across the front. Though now, there was quite a bit more damage.

I tossed it down and looked around. Something in the shadows of the bathroom caught my attention, and I got up and flipped on the light.

It wasn't a trick of the eyes. There was blood on the side of the tub and sink. It was dried, but definitely from the last twenty-four hours. I gripped the counter and leaned over, hanging my head as I tried to keep a clear mind. Bryer obviously needed me, and I wouldn't be any good to her if I lost it.

"What the fuck are you doing in here?" A man burst into the apartment.

I turned, ready to kill. It was the man from the wedding. Her boss. I stepped to him in two strides. Placing my arm under his chin, I pressed him into the wall and gripped his junk. "Where is she?"

He was an asshole. I knew it the night I met him, and I could smell it on him now. He might fool some people, but not me.

He gasped for air and clawed at my arm and hand. I pushed harder. "I'm really good at this, so I'll tell you how it will go. I'll release you as soon as I think you're gonna cooperate. I won't ask the same question twice."

His eyes widened, and while he stopped trying to remove my arm, he continued to attempt to pull my hand off his shriveled dick. I squeezed tighter.

I wasn't in the mood to play. Ripping my arm from his throat, I grabbed his hand and twisted until I had his face pushed up against the wall.

"Who the fuck are you?" He attempted to sound tough but failed.

"Really? You're gonna ask questions when I'm ready to cut your dick off for not giving me the information I need?" I growled, pressing him harder against the wall.

"You're in my daughter's apartment. I think I'm allowed to ask questions." He was almost whimpering now. His crotch had to hurt like a fucking snake bit him. I wasn't gentle.

His daughter? I would come back around to that later. "The wrong words are coming out of your mouth. I told you. I won't ask twice."

He sputtered and cried. "I don't know. She was here when I left last night."

"You saw her last night? Was she hurt?"

"I don't know!"

He was lying. I could taste it. I grabbed the knife from my thigh and held it to his throat. Slowly, I let it slide across his skin until a thin line of red emerged.

"Okay! Stop! Yes…" He cried. "Yes, she was hurt."

Fuck. "What happened?"

"She fell. But she was here when I left." He trembled under my hold.

There was more to his story. My intuition had never been wrong. That's what made me a great tracker. "When I find out what you're not saying, I will be back to resume this. What about Dani? Do you know where he is?"

Her friend might have answers.

"I don't know." The man shook violently. "But I have his number. It's on my phone. Back pocket."

Putting my knife in its sheath, I grabbed his phone and scrolled through contacts until I saw Dani's name and memorized the number. I wasn't going to use this fucker's phone. And I sure as hell wasn't going to text myself the info.

Never give an enemy your personal information. And until I knew more about this guy, he was an enemy.

I tossed his phone to the floor and grabbed mine. Dialing Dani's number, I continued to hold the man's arm behind him. He picked up on the third ring.

"This is Jax. I'm looking for Bryer, but she's not home. I know something happened, and I'm not in the mood for you to play any fucking game. Where is she?"

"Damn. Hello to you too. She's with Alice. Don't you think I would take care of her?" His usual snark hadn't been detoured by hearing my agitation.

It wasn't his job to protect her. It was mine, and right now, I was going to tear apart the fucking town to find her.

When I said nothing, he said, "Meet me at the city park, and you can follow me over."

"If you're trying to distract me, just remember I am fluent in torture." My attempt at civility had fled long before I entered this apartment.

The man currently under my hand whimpered again. "He's not kidding, Dani. Just take him to Bryer."

"Fuck. Is that Rick?" Dani grumbled something, and I could hear his engine start in his car. "Hit him once for me."

I let go of Rick, and he turned just in time to catch my elbow to the side of his face. He went down, and I crouched to make sure he was out. He lost consciousness and bodily functions. That happened more often than people expected. "When I have time, I'm coming back for you."

"Damn, what are you?" Dani's question had me chuckling.

"A beast." I hung up the phone and left Rick lying in a puddle of his own piss.

I made it to the park in record time. When I saw Dani's car, I pulled up behind him. Flashing my lights, I called him. "I'm here. Let's go."

It didn't take us long to drive to Alice's house near the outskirts of town. She lived in the newer homes away from the tree streets. It was a rather quaint part of town and not at all what I expected to be taken to.

I hardly had the truck in park before I jumped out and ran up the walk, pounding on the door. I could hear laughing and a TV on inside. While one might think that would be a good sign, it wasn't always in my line of work.

The door opened, and the girl from the restaurant stood there. Her smile widened when she saw me. "Oh, Bryer…" she said in a sing-song way. "Your sex god is here."

Her sex god? What the hell was that supposed to mean, and why was she acting as if I wasn't ready to tear her door down to find my woman?

She held the door open wider for me to enter. Looking in before taking a step, I saw Bryer curled up on the couch wearing my coat. Fuck.

I went to her. Dropping to my knees, I touched her face. "Are you okay, baby girl?"

Tears filled her eyes and silently fell down her cheeks.

"No, she's not." Alice picked up the remote and turned off the TV. "She hasn't told me everything, but I am pretty sure she's been abused for a long time."

Bryer's eyes widened. "Alice!"

"What? I'm not going to lie for some asshat. You were pushed down a fucking flight of stairs!" Alice stood there, arms crossed.

"What?" I gripped Bryer's hands to steady myself. "Is this true? Did someone push you?"

She nodded with more tears.

I wiped her cheeks and leaned in to kiss her. I regretfully pulled away from her lips to take her in. A small cut above her eye was a tad swollen.

"Stand up."

She looked over at Dani and Alice.

Dani stepped forward. "Jax, she's been through enough."

I glowered at him. "Is what Alice said true? Has she been abused?"

"*She* is right here." Bryer touched my face. "And yes. What she said is all true."

Dani glowered at me. "I brought her here last night after I found her in the tub."

As if my blood wasn't already boiling, he had to add that he saw her naked in the tub? Was she trying to kill herself? Was she drowning? I had so many new questions. My grip on her tightened. Fear wrapped around my heart and squeezed.

Bryer's jaw dropped as she realized Dani's mistake. "It's not what you think. He didn't know I was in there."

I clenched down on the toothpick and glared at him. "If you're so proud of yourself for helping her, why haven't you done it before last night? How long has this been happening?"

"It's not Dani's fault. He's helped me for years." She pleaded with me to understand.

But I didn't. I couldn't. Blood rushed so hard it roared in my ears. "Years?" I stood, unable to sit there with Dani standing so close. "It's taken you years to get her out of that house?"

Turning back to her, I noticed another cut. I lifted the hand I held, working to calm my tone as much as possible in the way I would speak to someone I'd just rescued. "Come on, angel. Stand up for me so I can look you over."

She winced as she moved slowly. Every movement made me hurt for her. I removed my coat. I was pleasantly thrilled with her finding comfort in something that was mine.

"Can you guys give us some privacy?" I stared pointedly at Dani. There was no way I was going to give him a pass. He might think what he did was protecting, but he was nothing more than a glorified Band-Aid. Someone there to offer first aid and maybe some comfort after a battle but nothing more.

Alice led Dani away from the living room, giving us the privacy Bryer needed. I'd been in plenty of situations and knew no one liked to be on display for an audience.

"I'm gonna lift your shirt, okay?"

She nodded.

Gently, I lifted the hem, stopping just under her breasts. Dark black and purple bruises covered her sides.

Tears filled my eyes and blurred my vision.

She began tugging out of her sweats until she stood in only her shirt and panties. A distinct pattern of bruises followed along her hips.

Fuck me.

I dropped back to my knees. I leaned forward and carefully rested against her stomach. "Forgive me, angel."

"You didn't do it."

"I wasn't here." I wrapped my arms around her and buried into her soft flesh. I let the tears fall freely without shame. "You're coming with me."

"Jax, I'm fine here."

"No." I stood and gripped her chin gently. Pressing my mouth to hers, I kissed her as if the kiss alone was a statement. "You are mine, and I protect what is mine."

She didn't understand my intense need to be around her right now. There was no way for me to leave her again.

She nodded. "Okay."

Good girl. I helped her pull on the sweats and made sure she was covered before hollering for Dani. "Go get all her stuff and meet me at the Dinner Station in two hours. She's coming with me."

"She's *my* roommate, buddy." Alice huffed. "You can't just manhandle her and dictate where she can and can't stay."

I chuckled. "I'm glad she has you as a friend, but I can guarantee I'm not leaving here without my woman. But she always has a choice. I would never force her to do anything. If she chooses to stay, so do I."

Alice gave her a worried look. "Bryer?"

"There's no place safer for me than with him. I'm gonna go with Jax." Bryer's voice was soft but confident. She would be getting praised for that later.

Alice placed a hand on her hip. "Your room will be here should you need it."

Dani shook his head. "What do you want? I already packed her a bag."

"Everything. She's not spending the night with me. She's moving in." I took Bryer's hand and felt her pulse pick up.

Dani clenched his fists at his sides. "Dude, she doesn't know you. I can't let this happen."

I wanted to laugh at his attempt to *stop* me. "I know it is fast, but I'd say it's reasonable under the circumstances. You see, there's a difference between you and me. You watched her get hurt for years. I refuse to let anyone hurt her."

"Dani, I know it might seem rash, but I've already decided I don't care. Okay?" She squeezed my hand, and I did it right back. I couldn't stop the slight grin from lifting the corner of my mouth. My girl was learning fast. "If age isn't a factor, then neither is time. I'm going with Jax."

Alice sighed like a sappy character off a show. "That's so sweet. Okay, Dani let's go. We got to pack up our girl."

"Oh no, you're not going over there with me." He shook his head.

She raised a brow, and her entire stance tightened. "Bet."

He cursed. "Whatever."

Bryer chuckled. I took her hand and brought it to my mouth, kissing it softly. "Let's go, angel."

She nodded. I picked her up and carried her to my truck. I made sure she was buckled and secure before turning to see Dani behind us.

"The Dinner Station is almost forty minutes out of town. Where are you taking her?"

"To Cardosa Ranch." I didn't wait for his response. He could ask just about anyone, and they would know about Jacob and his *ranchhands*. And by the look on his face, he didn't need to ask around.

In the truck, Bryer was shivering. I turned the key, set the heat on high, and pushed the button for her seat warmers.

Flecks of snow fell on the windshield as we drove, and I knew it wouldn't be long before we would be snowed in for the winter. It had been a long time since I had something so enjoyable to look forward to. But spending some snow-blanketed evenings cuddled up with Bryer on the front porch watching more snow lock us in had me thinking this might be the best winter yet.

I took her hand and held it tightly on my thigh. The adrenaline high was wearing off, and I felt halfway human and not so Hulk-ish. Not that I wouldn't rip someone's head off if they approached her right now.

"I'm sorry I didn't call. I wanted to. But I kind of broke my phone." Her gaze was on the passing landscape under the headlights as we drove.

"I saw that."

Her head snapped around, and her brows knit together. "You were at my apartment?"

I nodded and turned a corner. "I'd be lying if I said it didn't scare the living shit out of me. I saw the blood and the phone, and I worried something horrible had happened to you."

"What if it had? What could you have done?"

I pulled her hand to my mouth and kissed her knuckles, some of which were still red and swollen from her fall. "I would have burned the world down for you. Baby girl, I don't think you understand the extent of where I'd be willing to go for you."

"I'm hardly worth that kind of commitment." She looked back out the window. "Aren't you worried about going to jail?"

"No." I returned our hands to my thigh. "I told you. I am extremely good at what I do."

She didn't need to know how far my ties into the underground world went. One day, she'll find out, but that wasn't tonight. She needed to rest and heal. Her bruises were still fresh. God. I couldn't believe she was alive and not broken. But I'd have Doc look her over just to be sure.

I pulled my phone out and texted Diesel, letting him know my update. There's no need to keep him waiting on edge. I was sure he was at the computer following my every move. Damn trackers. Though... it wouldn't be a bad idea to get a pair of earrings for Bryer. It would have made today a hell of a lot easier.

"Rest, angel. I've got you now, and I promise you're safe. I won't let anyone hurt you." My words were spoken like a promise. One I intended to keep.

She leaned over, resting her head on my shoulder. "I know."

Kissing the top of her head, I drove us out of town. I had my angel, but the devil in me was ready to seek revenge on her behalf. I had a feeling those monsters she talked about were about to come out of hiding.

Chapter 14

Bryer

"I'll be right back, angel."

What? My groggy state of mind made it hard to understand what was happening.

I tried to process what I'd heard when a hand gently moved me to lean on a window. A jacket or something was placed under my head. I was so exhausted that I was fighting to stay awake.

The angle of my neck made my head begin to throb. I blinked. Where was I? Sitting up, I focused on the dash of Jax's truck. But I was alone and didn't know how much time had passed.

My heart raced as I spun to look around. Another set of headlights filled the empty parking lot of the Dinner Station.

Shit.

Where did Jax go? Who was out there with him? I wanted to check but was frozen in my seat.

A few thumps from the bed of the truck echoed in the cab. I peered into the darkness but couldn't see anyone.

A tap on my window had me yelping. I grasped at my chest and almost hyperventilated. Alice was on the other side of the glass, smiling and waving.

I rolled the window down. "You scared the shit out of me."

"Sorry. I just wanted to make sure sex god was being nice to you and to see if you changed your mind about going with him."

I offered her my best smile despite still trying to calm my heart. "I have never been more sure of anything in my life. I can't explain it. There's no logic to it. But he's my safe place. He's... he's home."

I knew I belonged with him when I saw him enter Alice's house. He found me. And then, when he went to his knees, my insides fluttered to the point I was sure my panties were soaked.

Maybe it was just attraction propelling me into rash decisions, but perhaps it was something else.

"And, his name is Jax, not sex god." I wasn't sure how to explain that one to him if he asked. At least, not without blushing.

She shrugged. "Same thing."

I rolled my eyes.

She leaned in through the window and gave me a quick hug. "Okay, looks like the guys are done loading your stuff. Text me when you get settled in. And if you need me... I'll drive up there, snow or no snow."

"Thanks, but I don't have a phone."

She gave a playful but exasperated sigh. "No, but your boyfriend does."

My boyfriend.

I had a boyfriend. It was such a foreign concept that I never thought about it.

Alice stepped back and waved. Dani joined her. "Hey, Bry. Day or night, if you need me—"

"I know," I cut him off. It had been the same since we were younger.

The driver's door opened, and I jumped.

Shit. I was really on edge. It felt like I was running away or escaping. Fear clamped down over my throat, and I tried to breathe but couldn't.

Jax took my hand and placed it on his thigh. I was quickly learning he liked to touch me. "Baby girl, I promise you're safe with me. No reason to be scared of anything with me around."

But what about when he wasn't with me?

After rolling my window up, we drove off. Leaving Dani and Alice behind in the dark was harder than I liked, but I felt oddly lighter. Without me to worry about, they could enjoy their evening.

"Where is this ranch you're supposedly taking me to? I've only lived here for about six years, so a lot of well-known families or places are still new to me."

"Where did you live before?"

"Idaho." I glanced out the window as I fought off a wave of demons threatening to appear. The thought of returning to Idaho and anywhere near our old house panicked me.

"Hey, where'd you go?" Jax's voice was soft but concerned.

I smiled. "I'm right here."

"No. In your mind. You went somewhere else." He picked my hand up and held it to his chest. "It will be my job to make sure you never return to wherever you went."

Good luck. "Don't take this wrong, but there are some monsters not even you could slay."

"Oh, angel, that sounds like a challenge."

I watched him for a moment. "Maybe it was."

His hand tightened around mine. "Challenge accepted."

Was this man real? Maybe when I fell, I hit my head, and I was in a coma, dreaming up this fantasy?

We drove to the cut-off by the lake and hooked a left onto a dirt road. I'd never been to the mountains up this way. Even in the dark, it was pretty. The sagebrush gave way to pine and juniper trees. And the snow forecasted to fall began in fat, fluffy flakes.

"The ranch starts here, but we won't reach the gate for a few minutes. These three mountains are part of Jacob's ruse to being a cattle rancher."

"So there are no cattle?"

He chuckled. "There are cattle, but he employs full-time men to handle that part of the business."

Everything about this man was interesting, but I didn't know enough to move in with him. I wondered if I was certifiably crazy. "So, have you worked here long?"

He twirled the toothpick in his mouth and gave me a playful side-eyed grin. "The ranch? I only help when I'm home. But I've worked for Jacob for almost eleven years."

That was a long time. It was strange to think he'd been in the same town as me for so long without ever running into each other. "What does it mean *when you're home?*"

"Usually, when we're hired to find someone, we are gone for a while. The last time ended up being two missions, and we were gone for almost three months."

I couldn't stop myself from frowning. I didn't like the idea of him leaving for so long. I hated the one night we were apart. Talk about separation anxiety. I probably needed therapy. Attaching myself to someone so quickly couldn't be healthy. Could it?

Maybe if they were *the* person.

Is that what Jax was? Was he *mine?*

"Hey, look at me."

I did as he said. I couldn't ignore him. I *wanted* to obey him in every way. I doubt there was anything I wouldn't do if he asked. His tone in *how* he commanded me had me eager to please him.

"I am a man who knows what he wants. I meant it when I said you're mine. I'm not going anywhere. If I leave… you have to go with me." His jaw flexed. "Bryer, I can't live a life where you aren't with me. I've seen things I can't erase from my mind that will keep me from letting you go too far. If you don't want me, fine, but just know that for whatever reason, my heart has found a purpose to beat with you, and I will always make sure you are safe. Even if you decide to leave, I won't be far away."

"I'm not gonna lie. This is moving fast. And yet, the last few days have been like a lifetime. If I said I wasn't scared, I'd be lying. I'm scared shitless right now." I laughed nervously. "I have spent my entire life hiding. Keeping secrets. Being utterly obedient to a fault. But leaving with you was the first time I ever wanted to do something for myself." I twisted to watch him under the glowing lights of the dash. "I didn't want to leave last night with Dani. He's asked me a thousand times to take off with him. But it was never right. He wasn't the one I was supposed to run to."

I sounded like a sappy romance novel, but if I was going to run away with my beast, then I was going to be honest. Not just with him, but to my heart—to myself.

"When you didn't call, all I could think of was that you were in trouble, and I wasn't there to save you." His face twisted as if in pain. "I can't do that again."

"Do what?"

He slowed to a stop and put the truck in park. "I lost someone once. It was what brought me to this life, this job." He squeezed my hand. "I have nightmares about it, but the night I met you, they changed. It was you I couldn't save."

My heart skipped a beat. "Who did you lose?"

"Her name was Alison. She was my little sister's best friend. I tried to save her, but…" He closed his eyes, and I knew he was reliving the moment. "She wasn't strong enough to handle what she went through. Her mind was gone before I could get to her."

I unbuckled and carefully scooted closer to him. It wasn't an easy task with all the bruises. My thigh brushed his, and I was acutely aware of how close I was to this man. "Jax."

His eyes opened, snapping to mine.

I touched his face, loving the feel of the rough stubble over his jaw. "I'm right here. I'm safe. And fuck the world and their time frames. It doesn't matter if we've known each other for five minutes or five years. I'm not going anywhere." I felt braver than ever. My heart beat so fast I wondered if it would explode. Leaning in, I took the toothpick from his mouth and pressed my lips to his.

His hand went to the back of my head, holding me to him as he deepened the kiss. The ache between my legs pulsed. I arched, unsure of how to find that release I needed.

My breast grazed his chest, but from this angle, it was hard to move to get more. I was too big to straddle him in the cab of a truck, but I wanted to feel him pressed against me.

My breathing hitched, and a moan escaped my throat.

"Fuck me," he said into my mouth. "I want to hear you do that with my cock inside you."

I was startled by his honesty, but the wetness between my legs increased. I'd never been so turned on in my life.

Maybe all we had was lust between us? My heart pitter-pattered, nearly shattering at the mere idea that that was all we had. Okay, so there was more. There had to be.

Instant attraction, we had in spades. But deep down, I knew he was everything I'd ever prayed for.

He leaned back first, his hands still fisted in my hair. "Baby girl, I need to get you to the ranch before I take you here in the truck."

"That would be highly unlikely."

His grip on my hair tightened as he pulled me closer. His breath was on my cheek. "Bryer, when it comes to you, nothing is unlikely. But our first time won't be on the side of the road. On the way to our wedding, absolutely. Parked outside of the church, with our friends and family waiting inside... I will fuck you until God Himself has to send you back down to me from the heavens because this devil will never let go of his angel. Not even in death."

Wedding? Was he talking about us in a long-term relationship that ended in marriage? But it wasn't the proposal/non-proposal that scared me. It was my willingness to let him do everything he said and more.

"Promise?" I barely heard my whisper.

His groan vibrated his chest. "Baby girl, you will be dripping with my cum as you walk down the aisle. You are mine, and I want to make sure you know where this is headed."

That pressure build-up I felt the night before in the tub returned, and I knew I was close to feeling whatever was on the other side of that mountain. Every inch of me was on fire and hyper-aware of Jax. I wanted him to touch me, to have his body mold against mine, to feel him inside me.

The wetness pooled in my panties, and I was sure there'd be a puddle on the leather seats if I moved.

He released me, waiting for me to move, but I couldn't. I had no desire to remove myself from his vicinity. "You better start driving then."

He smirked and put the truck in drive. I took the toothpick I'd stolen from him and placed it between my teeth, letting it roll over my tongue. I could taste him on the wood and almost moaned.

"Fuck." He slammed on the brakes and grasped my head, clamping down over my mouth, stealing the toothpick back. "You are gonna give me a heart attack doing that shit."

Playfully, I frowned. "Maybe I shouldn't be dating someone so old if I have to worry about your heart?"

"If you think you can ever date anyone but me, you're wrong." He flipped the toothpick with his tongue. "I'm gonna need to taste you on all my picks now. That gives me a few ideas."

My mind went to the dirtiest thing I could think of. There was no way he was thinking the same thing. I needed to get my mind out of the gutter before I was a seeping hot mess.

He put the truck back into drive, but I never moved. I loved feeling his leg against mine. He threaded our fingers together and held my hand on my thigh, inching higher.

I was going to die with how insanely turned on I was.

Chapter 15

Bryer

The entrance to the ranch was locked by a code. The iron gate was large enough that I wondered if Cardosa was trying to keep predators in or out.

Jax flashed a smile. "You can meet everyone that's here. Jacob and Lily are still on their honeymoon, and Bear left for a job, but everyone else should still be up, probably in the main house."

Meeting new people was not something I did well. My fight or flight kicked in, and I tensed.

He parked the truck next to a ginormous barn. Seriously, what could they keep in that thing?

One two-story house sat prominently above the other smaller, double-wides. It looked like there were about two or three single houses as well that sat off farther down.

Jax pointed to each. "That's the main house. It's where Jacob and Lily live. Those are our *bunkhouses*." He used air quotation marks. "But they are actually pretty nice. Bear, Diesel, Sam, and Fox live in that one. Flapjack and Callie live in the one next to it with me. The others are for the full-time ranchhands and their families." He pointed behind the main house. "And next month, Jacob is breaking ground on a couple more houses so we can each have one. Our family has been growing, and we need the room and privacy." He chuckled. "Trust me. Flapjack and Callie need the first house."

I followed, trying to remember everyone's names. "First question. Is Flapjack his real name?"

"No, his name is Carter, but he earned the nickname years ago because he's a damned good cook." He sat back and relaxed in the driver's seat.

The snow was falling heavily now, but he made no move to rush me out of the truck. I was grateful he was letting me go at my pace. "Second question. Where will I sleep?"

It was the most important question. I wasn't good with new places and needed to prepare myself the best I could.

"With me." He twirled the toothpick. "You can have the spare room if you'd like. I'll just sleep outside the door."

"Well, that's just creepy." I nudged him with my elbow. "What if…" I bit my bottom lip and almost lost my nerve to say what I wanted. "What if I wanted to stay in your room?"

He was the only one I knew, and I felt I would sleep much better if I was close to him. My unhealthy attachment was just getting worse.

He held his arm up for me to curl into his side. I moved a bit slower than usual, with my sides and hips yelling back at me for moving so much. But honestly, I wasn't hurting nearly as badly as I thought I would. Sore, yes. But nothing that would keep me from any normal activities.

He kissed the top of my head. "That's exactly what I hoped for."

I watched the snowflakes melt on the windshield. "How long are we staying out here?"

The heater was still running, but eventually, he'd have to shut the truck off.

"As long as you need. We can sleep out here for all I care. You are in charge of when we venture out and meet everyone."

It was sweet that he was willing to spend the night in the truck for me, but I couldn't do that to him. "What if everyone judges me? I'm young enough to be your daughter."

He chuckled, his chest vibrating with the laugh. "No one in that house will judge you. I promise." He wrapped his arm tighter around me but was careful of my side. "I'm gonna give you a little story, and then we'll see if *you* have any judgments."

I picked my head up slightly, but he pressed me back to his chest.

"I didn't say move. Just listen." His voice was deep and raspy, perfect for storytelling. "Jacob was the son of Everett Cardosa. He was the crime boss or kingpin for the western states. He started off running drugs and weapons through ports and cities. Eventually, he dipped his toes into trafficking. He was one of the biggest assholes to walk the face of the earth, from what I've heard. He killed Jacob's mother and had him help bury her. He was only seven."

I gasped. "That's horrible."

Jax chuckled. "It was, until it wasn't. Jacob swung the shovel and killed his dad. I think he matured faster because he had to. His aunt moved in to take care of him and their business, but by the time he was sixteen, he had taken over and decided he wasn't his father. He wanted to save people, not sell them."

"Well, I certainly can't judge Jacob. He sounds like a good guy. What do they call those? Anti-heroes?"

Jax smirked. "I'd like to hear you call him that and see what happens." His hand gently rubbed my side as he went on. "Lily was held captive for five years before we found her. It was actually me who stumbled upon her and watched her try to kill herself. That moment will live with me forever. But her story isn't mine to fully tell. I'm sure she will be happy to fill you in if you ask. You know... they have a bit of an age gap too."

I lifted my head. "They have seventeen years between them too?"

The rumble from his laugh vibrated his chest. "No. If I remember right, there are seven or eight years between them."

I relaxed back into his arms. "Yeah, no contest. Tell me about the others."

He rubbed my shoulder. "Diesel had a hard life. His girlfriend and baby were murdered, but he found love again with Sam, short for Samantha. Now *she's* someone you can judge. You see, she's a trained assassin. She worked for the cartel for years. It was either that or they would sell her body. She chose to kill instead."

I shot up, looking him dead in the eyes. "I couldn't judge her for that!"

He grinned, and I knew he was teasing me. "We aren't done with story time." He pulled me back down. "Where was I? Ah, yes… That brings me to Carter or Flapjack. He's messed up. Truly. And he can sneak up on a fucking rattlesnake, but he was also raised in the mafia along with his wife, Callie. She's a badass mafia princess. But she was subjected to some shit that could give you nightmares too." Jax shrugged. "We try not to judge them. Except for when the walls are thin, and angel, let me tell you, I haven't given them more than three stars yet."

I laughed and pushed at his chest playfully. "That's so wrong."

He dipped closer to whisper in my ear. "I'll have you screaming so loud they'll have to give us five stars." He gave my ass a swat. "Now stop interrupting me." He rubbed where he slapped. The sensation doing more than it should. "Bear is just a hard ass. But his bark is much worse than his bite. Winnie the Pooh is scarier than him. He has a story I'll let him tell, but I'm telling you, he is the one I would trust your life with the most if I were gone. He's like a blood brother. Don't get me wrong, there isn't a single one of them that wouldn't sacrifice their lives to save and protect you, but Bear and I are just—"

"Closer," I finished for him.

"Yeah. And last but not least, there's Fox. His name is actually London Fox, but we just call him Fox. His sister was sold, and he spent his teen years trying to find her. That's how he ended up with us. That last mission I told you about? The three-month one? We were looking for her. But it was too late. She'd died years ago. But that's also where Diesel met Sam. Hell, it's also when Flapjack got back together with Callie."

"You make them sound like heroes. Knights in shining armor, rescuing princesses from towers or fire-breathing dragons." I couldn't help but get a bit choked up. "I wished for you so long ago."

"I'm sorry it took me so long to find you." He sighed. "But I'm far from a fucking knight."

"I know, I know, You're a monster."

"I'm a beast. A devil. A monster. But never a knight." He kissed my head again.

I gripped his shirt, still not ready to move. "You told me their stories. But what about yours?"

"I was in the military. It was there I learned how good at tracking I was. I could find anything. Or anyone. But that's when Alison was taken. She was a reporter and found herself in the wrong place. She used my name, so they knew who I was." He took a deep, steadying breath. "I was ordered not to go, but I wasn't going to sit there and let her die without trying just because someone said *sit, stay*."

"You went AWOL?"

"Yeah. Ask me if I regret it."

"Do you?"

"No. I found her on my own, hours before they would have. But like I said, she was gone in her mind. It was too much. And when I was carrying her out of there, she grabbed my gun and shot herself." His chest shuddered with his breath. "I was court marshaled and was looking at a good many years in prison, but that's when Jacob found me and made a deal I couldn't pass up. But the people I killed, saving Alison, knew who I was and threatened to kill everyone I loved. So, I had to die."

"I don't understand." I gripped his shirt tighter. God, it must have been so hard for him.

"Jacob helped kill who I was and then took on the name Jax Harper. So, you can see why I was so scared when you didn't answer. I thought they'd found me and found out about you."

I scooted up to kiss along his jaw. "No one but you has me."

He pulled me close and just hung on. His pain wrecked my soul. All I could think about was telling him my story to show him he wasn't alone. I took a moment, afraid. I'd never told anyone of what I'd been through. Not even Dani knew all of it. He only knew I was being abused in some way. But sitting there with Jax, hearing their stories, I felt like maybe, just maybe, I really had found where I belonged. Kindred spirits and all.

I took a breath and tried to keep it steady as I exhaled. "When I was seven, my mother would put me in the bed of the man who molested me."

"Bryer." His body tensed.

"I listened. Now it's your turn. It's scary enough for me to do this, so just give me a minute. I've never told anyone what I'm about to tell you."

"Yeah, but you need to know I will kill everyone who has ever touched you." His tone was completely serious, and I believed him.

"I'm aware." My heart raced, and my fingers went numb.

"Just breathe, baby girl. You're safe." He ran a hand through my hair.

"That man was the first one I can remember. And eventually, it stopped. But then, when I was almost thirteen, my mom sat me down and explained how to give a proper blow job and then proceeded to tell me what would happen when a man goes down on me." I felt clammy and nauseous. Maybe, if I told him, I could start purging some of the demons I carried with me?

His arms tightened around me, and I was sure he stopped breathing.

"There was a boy... he was eighteen. He wanted to date me." I scoffed. "I thought it was innocent until my mom sent him to my room, and he shut the door."

"Bryer. I can't. Not without killing someone right now. If you tell me, he will die."

I ignored him. I needed to tell him. I had to get it out. "He started slow, but then each night, he got more and more rough until he forced my pants down and began licking. I can still hear the sounds he made. When he was done, he shoved his cock in my mouth and made me suck. I was only twelve."

The memories flooded me, and I grew angrier at my mom. "When I was fifteen, we moved, and I thought everything would be better, but it got worse. Guys were in our house left and right. She would send them my way, telling me to please them. Telling me how I was a whore and a slut and no one would want me, so this was the best thing I could do for her." Anger should have been what welled up in me, but the words my mother said to me were on repeat in my mind, almost as much as she used to say them.

I sniffed back the tears and choked on a sob. "It doesn't matter that I've only had sex once." I looked up at him. "That's the thing, it's only been one time. I never let the others, and they seemed fine, usually, as long as I got them off or let them touch me. But I can't help but feel that I'm ruined. I know I should have told you sooner." My tears soaked his shirt, yet I couldn't stop crying. I tried to move away from him, but he held me firmly to his chest. "I am not the kind of girl guys want. It's okay if you change your mind."

Jax opened the door without saying anything, and my heart dropped. He walked to the other side, snow sticking to his hair and shoulders before he could open the passenger door.

A feral look glazed over his eyes. Even in the dark, I could see the predatory stare.

He grabbed my hips, and I winced slightly as he pulled me to him. He stood with my legs on either side of him, with the door open, letting snow in and covering us both.

He wrapped his arms around me, burying his face into the crook of my neck. He stood that way, holding me until all my tears dried up. Running a hand down my hair and back, he continued to be my support. The tender actions melted the walls around my heart as if he truly was becoming my shelter from the world.

"I'm so sorry you had to survive that." His raspy voice warmed the side of my neck.

I clung to him, not wanting the moment to fade. I'd had a lifetime of fear and anxiety, but at that very moment, it was gone. Jax carried all of it, blocking me from the world and its monsters.

"Okay." I sniffed back that last tear and pulled away. The snow had fallen heavily, covering us both, and I laughed as I tousled his hair, letting it fall in clumps. "I know some of your secrets, and you know some of mine. We can decide right here, right now, if we move on or away from each other. Because I once heard a man say he decided right then he didn't care about something, and that kinda stuck with me. So, I'm making a decision that I don't care about your past. I don't care how many people you've killed, or *will* kill. I have decided I don't care."

His mouth crashed down on mine in a way I'd never experienced. It was rough and demanding. A growl emanated from his chest. He moved my legs, so they wrapped around him and then went to my back, pulling me closer.

I could feel his hardness through his jeans, pressing against my center. If he continued kissing me this way, I'd have my first orgasm in my sweats.

He pulled back, resting his forehead on mine. "You are not ruined. You are perfect. You are mine. I want you more than I ever thought it was possible to want another person. I've decided you are exactly what I want."

I released the world's longest sigh of relief. "You scared me when you got out of the truck but didn't say anything."

He pressed his forehead to mine. "I was trying not to lose myself and drive off to find every single one of those men *and* your mother..."

"I thought it was because you changed your mind." I wiped at the rogue tears still falling.

He took my hand and gently rubbed the tears away for me. "Never."

I leaned into his touch and closed my eyes. *Thank you, God, for finally answering my prayers.*

"I do have one question." He bent slightly to catch my eyes.

I looked up at him and nodded for him to go ahead. At this point, he knew more than anyone else. What was one more question?

"You said you've only had sex once?"

I nodded again. "About seven years ago. It was horrible, and with everything else in my life, sex was the farthest thing from my mind."

"Jax, is that you?" A man called from the porch of the main house.

I tensed and shied away from any attention this might bring.

Jax wrapped his arm over my shoulder and held me to his chest. "Yeah! Give me a few minutes."

"If that's all it takes for you!" The man called out with a chuckle.

"Damn asshole." Jax rubbed my back. "We all have a past, angel. Mine is tainted in blood. I told you I wasn't a good man, yet here you are. I've already decided to make you mine. Nothing changes."

"You know, when Beauty ran away from the Beast, that's when she ran into the wolves." I wrapped my arms around his middle and held myself to him. "He saved her, and then they fell in love."

"Are you saying you love me?"

"Not yet."

"Hum, so then you're saying you're gonna run, and I have to chase you? Because let me just say, that won't end the way you think it will." His cock pulsed between my legs.

"I have a feeling you are way more beast than man."

He growled, "I'll give you a three-second head start if you want to find out."

I didn't think I could get any wetter but hearing him growl and basically telling me to run was doing things to my insides. My clit was so sensitive the slightest movement would have me moaning.

My heart pounded in my ears. "Give me five seconds."

A mischievous twinkle sparked in his eyes, and his mouth curved. "Run, beauty."

Oh, shit.

He moved to the side and let me escape the truck. But I didn't know where to go. There was a tree line past the houses that looked like the best place to hide.

My hips protested almost as much as my sides, but I could feel him watching me. Counting down. Ready to hunt me. It was sick how excited I was about it all.

The adrenaline urged me forward. Past the tree line and into the woods, I could hear him gaining on me.

The snow fell in tuffs, covering the ground. It also made it harder to see where I was going.

"What Beauty didn't know was that the Beast was watching her the entire time, and he wasn't about to let her go." Jax's voice echoed around me.

I ducked behind a tree. "Maybe that's what she wanted?"

"Oh, angel, you always say the right things."

I spun and ran right into Jax. His solid chest was a wall of muscle. "Hello, baby girl."

I squealed as he scooped me up, only to set me in a pile of leaves and snow. My breathing was heavy, but he was steady, as if he didn't just run into the woods after me.

His mouth claimed mine in a fiery demand. His hands roamed over my body, rough but gentle over the bruises. He reached under my shirt, grazing my bare stomach, inching higher.

I arched, anticipating his touch. Thankfully, I didn't have a bra on.

It felt like forever until his hand cupped my breast. I whimpered when he pinched my nipple, and it hardened immediately. He flicked and then rubbed it, circling the sensitive peak.

He stopped kissing me to pick me up, taking my shirt off in one swoop. Then, he quickly took the nipple in his mouth. I cried out as shocks of pleasure went through me.

He played with the other breast while sucking and licking the one he'd captured. God, how could something feel so good? I had been so desensitized to touch before him it was like I was in an entirely different body.

"Jax," I called out.

I gripped his hair as he bit down, growling. "I am preparing my feast, little wolf."

My head whipped back and forth as he continued his attention to my breasts. It was too much. I felt it building in me, and there was no way to release it.

He sat back on his heels and gripped the waist of my sweats. "I need to hear you say it, Bryer."

"Yes." I nodded and lifted my hips to allow him to remove the clothing.

"You need a safe word. I won't go further until you give me something you can say to stop me if you need."

"God, I can't think. Jax… please."

"Not without a safe word. Something you'll remember."

"Fuck. I don't know. Poprocks!"

He chuckled. "Poprocks?"

"Why not? Are candies not allowed?" My chest heaved with each breath.

"Anything is allowed, little wolf. I just figured you for a chocolate girl." He tugged at my sweats without breaking eye contact. "Poprocks it is. You say it when or if you need me to stop, and I will immediately. I won't be mad or upset if you use this word. But if you need me to stop, say it. Don't hesitate. Do you understand?"

I nodded.

"Good girl."

Hearing him call me a good girl made me wetter.

He carefully removed the pants, mindful of my hips. The snow melted on my feverishly bare skin immediately. He slid a finger under the leg band on my panties. I squirmed, wanting more.

"My beauty is impatient."

"Maybe this is a good time to tell you I've never orgasmed before. So it's okay to just do what you need."

"Not ever?"

I shook my head, whimpering as he inched his way to my center.

"Not even by yourself?"

Again, I shook my head.

His grin widened. "But you admit you've touched yourself?"

I nodded. "Once. Last night." I gasped as he grabbed my panties and began slipping them over my hips.

"Just once?"

"I was close, but then Dani—"

Jax captured my mouth with his. "I don't like hearing another man's name fall from your pretty lips. Just for that, I'm going to punish you. One day I'm going to fuck you until the only name you scream is mine." He bit my bottom lip and then gently ran his tongue over it. "But make no mistake. I'm the only one who can ever punish you, and I promise it will always be in ways that bring you pleasure."

I groaned into his mouth.

He got up, the snow from his hair falling onto my body as he shifted to finish taking my panties off. I shivered. But it wasn't the cold. I was completely naked and aware of his eyes on every curve. I tried to cover myself with my hands, but he grasped them and held them tightly above my head.

"You're so fucking beautiful. I will never tire of looking at you. If you ever try to hide from me again, I will tie your hands to our bed and make you come until you pass out." He leaned in to grasp a hard nipple in his mouth. "And then I'll keep going until you wake up and start again."

I bucked under his mouth. God, the way he talked...

Fuck. I'd never heard anyone say those things. But I believed him. I was naked in the woods during a snowstorm, so tying me to a bed didn't sound too far-fetched for him.

His free hand slid lower. I tensed as he reached the curls between my legs. I wasn't one of those bare girls and was suddenly self-conscious.

"Maybe you shouldn't go there." I whimpered as he slid a finger over my clit.

"Are you saying your safe word, angel?"

I shook my head. "No. I just..." I moaned as he stroked the delicate spot. "I'm not... bare. It's not..." Fuck, he had to stop moving his fingers so I could talk. "You don't have to."

Jax chuckled darkly. "Baby girl, this right here belongs to me." He let go of my hands, but I kept them where he had them. He pushed my legs open and crawled between them, grabbing under my knees and lifting. "If you ever wax or shave it bare, I will punish you."

He kissed along my thigh. He was so close to that part of me. The part that I hated for so long.

I worried I wouldn't be able to handle it and push him away, but the closer he got, the more I felt myself dripping.

"My little wolf looks like she's enjoying this."

The snow came down harder, but I didn't care. The icy flakes cooled my heated body. The hot-cold difference spiked the intensity as the snow fell on my exposed breasts.

He buried his face at my entrance, licking and tasting every drop. I grabbed his hair and arched to feel more. Holy shit. What was that feeling?

A finger slipped inside me, and I tensed, waiting for the pain, waiting for the repulsion to set in, but there was nothing but pure blissful pleasure. Jax was like a drug, and I wanted more. I needed to feel more.

I writhed under him, and he pressed down on my stomach, holding me to the forest floor. He growled as he feasted on me.

The tightness returned until I thought I would break into a thousand pieces if something didn't happen. Or maybe I needed to shatter to find myself?

"Let go, baby girl. I've got you."

He licked my clit and thrust a second finger inside, curving up and hitting a spot that stole my vision. I curled into him, screaming his name.

I broke. Falling over the precipice and shattering my soul. I clung to Jax's shoulders while he continued to lap up the sweetness I released.

I felt the tightness build almost immediately again, and I arched under him, begging for the next wave to take me away. I cried out, my throat raw from yelling.

"Jax," I pleaded. For what I didn't know. I only knew he was the one to give me what I needed.

The second orgasm washed over me, leaving me shaking and gasping for air. Jax looked up at me with a devilish glint in his eyes as his tongue licked me ever so slowly. With our eyes locked, I watched him greedily devour my clit. "Keep watching me." His hot breath warmed where his tongue continued to tease.

His eyes glossed over when I whispered his name. His fingers thrust inside me, finding that magical spot.

"One more, angel."

I didn't think it was possible. My mind swam in delicious pleasure. I shook my head.

"One more," he repeated with a growl.

One more swipe of his tongue sent me reeling over the edge into nothing. The world went dark, and I wasn't sure if the scream was from me or a wild animal, but I didn't care.

Jax snaked up my body, crashing his mouth on mine. I could taste myself on his lips, and I licked every drop off him, making him groan. Why was it so arousing to suck my wetness off his lips?

This man had given me not only my first orgasm but three of them. And I still wanted more. I craved more.

I wound my arms around his neck and pulled him to me.

He kissed me until I couldn't breathe, then trailed to my neck, where he sucked and nibbled along my collarbone, leaving little marks, I'm sure.

I shivered again, but this time, it was the cold setting in. It didn't matter how feverish I was a minute ago. I was feeling the effects of the snow now.

Jax scooped me up and set me on his lap. It was hard to pretend I couldn't feel his rock-hard cock pressing against my ass through his jeans.

He took off his shirt and slipped it over my head. The warm article immediately felt like being wrapped in a cocoon. Standing up, he carried me toward the houses.

I tucked myself into his chest and tried not to freak out that he was carrying me. I wasn't exactly light. But also... I only had on his shirt. What if his family saw me like this?

"I'm not sure I can meet everyone tonight."

"That's good because we're going to my room, where I'm gonna finish what we started. You can meet them in the morning."

I knew he couldn't see my blush, but it warmed my cheeks. I wasn't sure anything could ever feel as good as what he just did to me, but I was excited to find out.

For the first time in forever, I felt like me. The me I hid from everyone, even myself. The me I protected from the world and all the people in it. So, how in the hell did Jax find *that* me?

I closed my eyes and took in the moment I became alive.

Chapter 16

Jax

I licked my lips and groaned. I could still taste Bryer on me. She was in my mouth, on my lips, my fingers... My cock throbbed, and I desperately wanted to bury it deep inside her.

I carried her to the edge of the forest, but I bypassed the truck and went straight to my bunkhouse. The lights were off, which meant Flapjack and Callie were still at the main house. Good. I didn't want my little wolf to muffle any of her sounds.

I kicked my bedroom door shut behind us and then locked it for good measure. Setting Bryer on the edge of the bed, I lifted my shirt from her. She shivered, but it wouldn't take long before she warmed back up. She had been such a good girl, letting me chase her and then feast between her legs out in the open. God, I could die between her thighs, and I'd be happy.

But I had no plans on dying anytime soon. Not when I had a lifetime to make this woman scream my name. I stood back and looked at her. Shit. She was like a goddess. I wanted to memorize every curve, every soft inch of her, every dimple.

I whipped off my belt and tossed it to the floor beside the bed in case we needed it later, but I left my jeans on. "Still no safe word?"

She shook her head.

"Crawl up there and spread your legs for me."

She inched back, taking her time to get in position. She better hurry, or I might need that belt sooner than I thought. My cock strained against the restraints of the tight material, and I felt the hot wetness as pre-cum dripped from my tip. I was lucky I didn't shoot my load in my jeans when she came the last time. Hearing my name fall from her lips as she peaked did things to me I couldn't explain.

She was up on the bed but didn't spread her legs. "I want to see you dripping, baby girl."

Her cheeks turned crimson as she tentatively opened her legs.

"Wider." I watched as she spread her legs, giving me the best view on earth. She was so wet.

Tonight was all about her. I wanted her to experience how, if a man truly cared about his woman, he would always do whatever she needed to feel loved, beautiful, and worthy.

But being the one to give her pleasure had my cock so hard it would take a few cold showers with my hand to get it to go down. The way she writhed under my touch, the husky sounds she made, my name falling off her tongue with a cry as she came.

My cock twitched.

"You were such a good girl for me. I want to reward you again." I kneeled on the end of the bed between her ankles.

"What about you?"

"Angel, you *are* my reward." I flashed her a rogue grin and picked her leg up, kissing the inside of it. "There's not a part of you I don't want my lips to touch. Every inch of you should be kissed and worshiped."

She tensed as I got closer to her entrance. Her breathing picked up. "Jax. I don't think I can go again."

"I don't hear a safe word." I continued kissing her, letting her small sounds guide me to where she needed to be kissed most of all.

Fuck. Her pussy was so wet. She dripped for me. I licked and sucked, not wanting to waste a single drop. If heaven had a flavor, it would taste like this. I growled as I fucked her with my tongue. Her heat enveloped me, and her sweetness filled my mouth. I rubbed her clit. My cock twitched as she moaned.

Burying my face between her legs, I needed to be deeper. I wanted to lap up everything she had to give me. I wanted to feel her come and drink her down.

Moving my tongue to her clit, I pressed my fingers inside her. Stretching around two fingers, her walls were tight, but I felt her shudder and clench around me.

I couldn't wait to bury my cock in her sweet pussy. I wanted to fill her with me and release inside of her. I would need to make sure she was ready for me, stretching her with my fingers before taking me in. She wasn't used to anything, and I wasn't exactly small by any man's measure. It wasn't cocky, but I knew my seven inches was above average, and I would need to go slow with Bryer.

But that was a plan for another night.

She gripped my shoulders, moving and arching under me. As if I were dying of thirst, I craved her release. She tensed, tightening around my fingers, and I knew she was close. I hooked my fingers up and caressed the spot I knew would make her come.

Her cries filled the room as she clawed my bare skin. I didn't let up. I was a crazed man with a need to see her become delirious from pleasure.

"Jax!" Tears fell down her cheeks. Her head whipped back and forth, and she moved her hands from my shoulder to the blankets under her, gripping and tugging on them as she tightened and came again.

I sucked her sweetness down, drinking as if she were an oasis in a desert. She shuddered and cried out, whimpering my name over and over. It was like a hit of heroin, and I needed more to edge me off my craving.

Her chest rose and fell in heavy swells as she gasped for air. If two fingers had her coming, maybe three would continue the wave.

I stretched her open, inserting one more.

She moaned, lifting her hips for me. God, all I wanted to do was keep rewarding her. Her legs tightened around me, trying to close, but I spread her wider, holding her open, and growled. "Little wolf, this beast isn't done feasting."

"Jax. I can't." Her panting only spurred me on.

"One more, angel. Give me one more." I ravaged her pussy, licking, sucking, and thrusting my fingers deep inside.

She screamed as her body convulsed, forcing a mouthful of cum into my mouth. I sucked, taking it all. My cock jerked, and I knew I was seconds from coming in my jeans.

I sat up, giving her a reprieve and watching her fall. Her eyes were glossy, full of heat. Her body shook, and her chest shuddered as it rose. Fuck, she was absolutely stunning.

She lay limp, trying to catch her breath.

I tugged off my jeans, leaving my boxers on despite the raging hard-on I had, and crawled up onto the bed beside her. Pulling her to me, I wrapped my arms around her and kissed her head. "You were such a good girl."

My cock strained, aching with a throbbing need as it pushed against her ass, but I wasn't about to leave her side to find my own release.

She found my hand and threaded her fingers with mine, bringing them to her mouth and kissing my knuckles. "I don't have words right now, so if I forget to say it later, thank you."

I chuckled. "Angel, you don't have to thank me for eating your pussy." If anything, I should be thanking her.

She yawned and laughed, swatting at my hand. "No. It's more than that. It's everything. It's being here. It's your arms. It's the orgasms. It's how you make me feel."

"And how do I make you feel?"

Finally, her breathing slowed. She relaxed in my arms. "Safe." Her whisper was nothing more than a faint sound as she fell asleep.

I still needed to clean her up but didn't want to move. I didn't know I was missing anything in life as much as this until now.

Baby girl, I'm gonna love you. I don't know how or when, but I will make you love me too. And I will protect you like you've always deserved. Nothing will stop me when it comes to you. I rubbed her bare back, loving how soft she felt under my fingertips.

She roused, wincing as she shifted to look back over her shoulder at me. "Is there a bathroom I could use?"

It concerned me she was still in so much pain. I shouldn't have chased her. "I'll take care of you. Stay right here. I'll be back."

She grabbed my arm. "That's very nice of you, but I'd still like to *use* one. It's been a while since Alice's house."

Shit. She wasn't wrong. Getting up, I found a T-shirt in my drawer for her to wear. "You are *not* allowed to go out there naked."

I got up and took her hand, helping her from the bed, and then walked her to the bathroom. "I'll wait here. I need to use it too."

It felt so natural having her there. Waiting turns for the restroom before heading back to bed. Something about it had me needing her even more.

She opened the door, and I braced my arm on the doorframe, preventing her from leaving. I snuck a hand under the shirt and pushed it between her legs. She grabbed my shoulders and whimpered.

"Jax, what are you doing?"

"I want to see you come all over my hand." I spread her with my fingers and stroked her clit. Her body trembled, and I felt her growing weaker, barely standing.

Her fingers dug into my skin as she attempted to stay on her legs. "I can't." She panted, with small moans escaping with each breath. I loved the little noises she made.

"You haven't said your safe word, so I'm not stopping." Fuck, I could watch her come a million times, and it wouldn't be enough.

She tipped her head back and reached out to cling to the doorframe. "Jax!"

"Come, baby girl."

Her body shuddered as she fell apart. I held her until she could come back to me. My hand pulled away, glistening with her cum. I licked my fingers, sucking her from me. Fuck, I would never be able to stop doing this with her. She was more potent than a drug. Nothing could compare to her.

A deep red flushed her skin as she tried to straighten herself. Her glossy eyes drooped, and she yawned. It was so cute that I wore her out.

"Go to bed. I'll be right there." I kissed her head and gave her ass a pat as she passed.

After I used the restroom, I grabbed a warm cloth to take care of Bryer and then stopped by the kitchen to grab a bottle of water and some painkillers for her. Doc made sure we had an ample supply before he took up retirement.

When I returned to the room, she watched the door with wide eyes, almost as if she were afraid of what or who might come through it.

"Baby girl, I don't care which side of your body you sleep on, but I sleep on the left side of the bed."

I let my gaze roam over her body. She was still in my shirt, but that only turned me on even more. I couldn't explain it but having her in my things made me hard. At this rate, I'd be fucking her every thirty minutes.

She didn't move but watched me curiously. "Why?"

That was easy. "Because if anything or anyone ever comes through that door, they have to get through me to get to you. I sleep between you and our enemies."

I handed her the pills and water. "Take these while I clean you up."

"I kinda did that already." She sat up and swallowed every last drop.

I sat beside her and pushed her legs open. "That is my job, angel. You will learn that I take care of everything that is mine." Slowly, I drew the rag over her. It wasn't supposed to turn sensual, but she made a small noise, and her body tightened as I wiped over her entrance and clit. Leaning in, I kissed her thigh. She sucked in a breath.

I tossed the rag into the basket of dirty clothes across the room and pulled the blankets down. "Get in."

She obeyed quickly, scurrying under the covers.

I checked my nightstand, ensuring my gun was where it needed to be. I had a few hidden around the room, but this one was the easiest and quickest to reach.

Laying under the covers with her, I held my arm out so she could curl up with me. My arm went around her, and she laced her fingers with mine, holding me to her chest. I kissed the back of her head. "Sleep. I've got you. You're safe." From everyone but me.

"Fuck!"

"Jax!"

I jolted awake and reached for my gun. Bryer was already sitting up and staring at the door, her chest heaving and eyes wide.

"Stay here. Lock the door behind me." I slipped from the bed and closed the door, waiting only for a split second to hear the lock engage. *Good girl.* "Flapjack?"

The way he was yelling was like we were under attack. I had a million scenarios racing through my head and tried to find a way to make sure I saved Bryer in each one.

"Fuck, fuck, fuck!" Flapjack was in the kitchen, lacing his thigh sheath full of throwing knives to his leg.

"What's going on?" I kept my gun cocked and ready.

"It's Bear." He opened the drawer of ammo. "His plane went down somewhere in Idaho." He grabbed handfuls of boxes and slammed it shut. "Fuck!"

I uncocked my gun and carved a hand through my hair. Son of a bitch. My heart dropped. "Is he okay?"

"We don't know."

I followed him to his room, where Callie was already packing a bag for them. "What do we know?"

Callie shoved more ammo than clothes in her bag, taking a few boxes from her husband. "The plane went down somewhere in the Sawtooths. There is no response from the plane. No transmitter. Nothing. Bear's phone is either dead or there's no service."

"What about his tracker?"

Flapjack cursed again and zipped his bag before hanging his head. "It stopped at the same time the plane went down. Nothing. It hasn't moved."

"It doesn't mean he's dead. He could be staying with the plane. He knows we'll come for him." God, no. Bear was my brother through and through. My best friend. My heart shattered as I imagined the worst. "I'll be ready in five minutes."

Flapjack looked up. "I'm leaving in four."

He was the best driver out of all of us, and I wasn't going to argue that I could drive too. We all dealt with shit differently. "I have Bryer. I can't leave her."

Callie cocked her head. "Under different circumstances, I'd be thrilled, but I have to ask. Is it smart to bring her?"

I knew Callie had her own demons that controlled her thoughts. She and Flapjack had been through them together.

I clenched my jaw. "She's coming."

"Fuck, I don't care. She'll be family one day anyway." Flapjack sucked in a sharp breath to steady himself. "If she's here with you, she already is."

I darted to my room and rapped on the door. "Bryer? Baby girl, it's me. I need you to open up for me."

The door unlocked, and she stepped back. Standing in nothing but my shirt, I realized I had never brought in her things last night.

"We have to go. I'll grab a bag for you, but we need to dress quickly."

"What's going on?"

"Bear's plane crashed. We're gonna go find him."

Her hand went to her mouth as she gasped. "Jax. I'm so sorry."

I left her there, unable to accept any sympathy, worried I would jinx Bear's predicament. He was fine. He had to be. I would know it if he was dead.

I pictured my mother and sister at my funeral. They thought I'd died and didn't know I had only been a few feet away.

This was different.

I ran outside in my boxers to grab Bryer's bag. The snow had stopped sometime during the night, leaving a few inches on the ground.

Racing back to the room, I found Bryer naked, reaching for the bag.

"Shit, woman, what are you doing?"

"You told me to hurry. I wasn't going to waste time."

"One, other people in the house could have walked in and seen you. I wouldn't be okay with having to remove my brother's eyes. But two, you are getting rewarded later for obeying so well." I pulled on my jeans and boots. Grabbing a shirt, I tucked it in and looped my belt around my waist.

She was faster than me. "I'm ready except for shoes. I think we left those in the woods last night. I have some boots in my suitcase, though, if you can grab them?"

I didn't hesitate and rushed to grab her suitcase and another bag. I wasn't sure what was in any of it. In the house, Callie and Flapjack were nearly ready. I dropped the luggage on our bed. "Pack one bag, everything you might need. I don't know how long we'll be gone. But make sure you have warm things."

I grabbed my large duffle from the closet and shoved clothes in. I had a drawer of knives and picked out three, along with a few guns and ammo. We never went anywhere without packing.

When I turned, Bryer stood there with her bag hanging from her hands. I grabbed it from her and tossed it with mine over my shoulder.

Giving her a quick kiss, we bolted from the house.

Everyone was outside loading into the trucks. Bryer shimmied up behind me, almost hiding from them. It wasn't the most conventional time for introductions, but I didn't want her to feel unwanted or unwelcome either.

Diesel gathered everyone together. As Jacob's second hand, it was his job to make sure we were all briefed.

"Bear's plane lost all communication before it went down. We don't know if there was a malfunction, if it made an emergency landing, or crashed. His tracker went down with the plane and hasn't moved. But it's active, so I have hope that just means he's staying with the aircraft. We will *not* assume Bear and the others are dead. Until there is confirmation otherwise, we will proceed as an extraction." Diesel took Sam's hand. "We don't leave one of our own." He looked at me, then to Bryer. "And it looks like we've grown overnight. I'm sorry you had to meet us this way, little sister."

I pulled my angel close to my side. "This is Bryer. That's Diesel and his girl Sam, Flapjack and his wife Callie, and our youngest brother, Fox."

"Don't worry, it's all intense and overwhelming at first, but then you'll get used to it and realize all these guys are like the big brothers you never had." Sam looked away, wiping a tear from her cheek.

The uncertainty of Bear's predicament weighed heavily on us all. Our brother was in trouble.

Diesel tapped the side of the truck bed. "Alright, let's load up. Flapjack, you have Callie, Jax, and Bryer. Fox, you're with me and Sam."

We piled into the trucks. I went to move in next to Bryer, but Callie jumped in and gave me a coy smile before shutting the door.

Sliding into the passenger front seat, I looked back at Bryer, who looked like a wild animal ready to flee at the first chance she got. I knew it was all new to her, but going slow wasn't an option now.

There was no way in hell I was going to leave her. Before I felt comfortable enough to let her stay without me in town, I needed to take care of a few things, or rather a few people. Her stepfather wasn't going to be around much longer, I could guarantee that. I wasn't sure what to do with her mom. I wasn't in the habit of harming women. But what she did to Bryer was beyond acceptable, and I wasn't above killing *anyone* who ever touched or hurt my beauty.

Chapter 17

Bryer

"Where did you meet Jax?" Callie dove right into the interrogation like a pro.

Jax said she was the daughter of some mafia boss, so maybe she was?

"At the wedding. I was one of the servers for the catering." I fiddled with my fingers, hoping for easy questions.

"How old are you?"

"Callie," Jax's stern voice was a warning. I wasn't sure how I knew, but I knew.

"What?" Callie's well-manicured fingers gripped the front seat as she scooted closer to the guys, poking her head through the center. "You ask any guy out there, and he'll tell you it's the sister's job to make sure the girl dating her brother is acceptable."

Flapjack chuckled. "Amore, I can assure you, if Jax brought her home, he's already decided she's the one."

Jax glanced back at me. "I promise, there is nothing you could say or do to change my mind about her."

I ducked my head to hide the blush.

Callie sat back in her seat. "Oh, I don't want to change your mind. I just want to make sure she knows what she's getting into with such an old man. Women have to stick together, let each other know there are options and plenty of fish in the sea." She held a finger up to her lips and winked. "I wouldn't want Bryer to think she has to settle for shriveled dick when she could be... oh, I don't know... with someone younger? Like Fox! Oh, I bet she'd love him."

"Callie," Jax's growl deepened.

151

She leaned her head back on the headrest. "I only have so much sarcasm on reserve right now. It's how I cope. You, of all people, should remember that."

She rolled her head so she could look at me. "He was the one who helped me the most when Carter was taken. Poor guy. He got the brunt of all my moods."

Jax scoffed. "All your moods or your personalities?"

She shrugged. "Same thing."

Jax's laugh filled the truck. "Yeah, I remember one of those personalities when I had to carry you from that house."

I gasped, completely taken aback, looking from Callie to Jax. "Wait. You carried her from a house?"

"I wasn't going to leave Carter. But Jax made me. And then what happened?" She sat up, grabbing the seat in front of her to lean in toward the guys again.

Flapjack gave her a look that spoke volumes from the rearview mirror. "It was better me than you."

She scoffed. "I'll die on this battlefield. Watching them take you nearly killed me."

Her husband reached back, taking her hand. It was kinda sweet to see them interact. "And if it were reversed, it *would* have killed me. After I killed Jax for not getting you out of there."

She rolled her eyes but never let go of him. "So you keep saying."

Jax saved Callie… and Flapjack took her place. I think. It was confusing to follow their stories when there were so many. Jax told me a few things before, but I didn't expect them to talk about it as if it were so normal. Like this was an everyday occurrence or event.

"Why was it Jax and not someone else?" I asked Callie.

"Because." She let go of Flapjack to slug Jax in the shoulder. "He was the one Carter trusted the most with me."

"Yeah, and then you bit me." Jax turned and held his arm out. "I'm lucky I didn't scar."

She shrugged. "But you didn't."

He smirked. "And then you scared the shit out of me when you weren't where you were supposed to be. Damn. Flapjack *would have* killed me."

Knowing what I knew about his past, I worried he would have killed himself over losing another girl.

"You see, Bryer," Flapjack looked at me through the rearview mirror. "There's a code between us. This family is tighter and stronger than blood could ever make us. We might be murderous assholes, but we protect our own. And you come first."

Callie leaned toward me to whisper, "He means all of us women. There's something extremely sexy and empowering to know you're on a pedestal so high God has to look up to see us."

Jax's heated gaze locked with mine, and then he winked. "I told you, there's no place safer than with me."

I was beginning to understand he wasn't lying.

The headlights illuminated the large Welcome to Idaho sign along the highway, and my stomach lurched. I guess somewhere in the bustle of the morning, I didn't understand we would be *going* to Idaho.

I couldn't breathe.

The memories I couldn't erase clamped around my throat, restricting air from getting to my lungs. I gripped the seatbelt and pulled it away from me. I wanted to open my chest up and let oxygen in.

"Um, Jax…" I heard Callie's voice but was too caught in my head to pull myself out.

"Baby girl, look at me." Jax twisted in his seat, leaning through the middle to reach me. He gripped my chin and forced me to look. "Bryer. Breathe."

I gasped. My body shook.

I couldn't go back to Idaho.

"What's going on?" Flapjack looked concerned but never slowed down.

He needed to stop and let me out. I'd walk back if I had to. I couldn't go back to that place.

"I don't know. Pull over for just a minute. Callie, switch with me."

Flapjack pulled off onto the dirt shoulder. I didn't have time to escape because Jax got out, and Callie crawled over the center console and into the front seat before Jax got in next to me and closed the door. We were stopped for maybe three seconds before Flapjack sped off, the tires flinging dirt and rocks as he reentered the highway.

Jax unbuckled me and pulled me to his lap. His arms wound around me, holding me to him. The steady beat of his heart became my focus until my breaths matched his. Slow and steady.

His thumb caressed my back. "Tell me how to help." His words were low and meant only for me.

The panic subdued, and I buried my face into his shirt. "I'm so embarrassed."

He continued to rub my back. "Why?"

"Because I freaked out," I squeaked into his chest. "I promise I'm not always so crazy and emotional." It seemed to be that since meeting him, every emotion possible has flooded me at some point.

"First." He tipped my chin up. "You're not crazy. But it would help if I knew why you freaked out."

I sat up straighter and played with the buttons on his shirt. "I haven't been back here in years. It was like all the memories crashed down on me at once."

"I understand that." He reached into a pocket and pulled out a pack of toothpicks, placing it between his teeth. "It's why I carry these."

He twirled it over his tongue, moving it back and forth.

Jax offered me one. "It gives your mind something to focus on when all the demons try to come in."

I took the toothpick and clenched it with my lips. I felt silly, but he wasn't wrong. It gave me something to focus on.

I sighed, leaning back into him. "Jax, you can't save me from everything."

He stilled, his lips grazing my head. "I have to."

Life was constantly surprising me. One day, I was catering a wedding, dreaming of someone to save me, and the next day, I was rescued by a vigilante. I smirked. My knight in shining armor wore a cowboy hat and boots.

I twisted so I was sideways on his lap. He held me with one arm, letting me sink against his chest and resting my head on his shoulder. Never in a million years did I think I would be so comfortable sitting on anyone. I worried I would crush them. But Jax didn't seem fazed by my weight, giving me confidence.

He put his hand on my knee, rubbing soothing circles with his thumb.

Callie twisted to check on us. Her grin softened. "Seeing him happy means everything to us."

"His last girlfriend didn't make him happy?" I hated to think of anyone hurting Jax. He had a good heart and meant well. He would kill for someone he loved.

"Last girlfriend?" Callie looked confused. "Sweetie, I was beginning to think he was dating his hand."

Flapjack half coughed, half laughed. "Bryer, what my beautiful wife is trying to say is that Jax hasn't dated anyone since we've met him."

"Thanks for giving my history lesson." Jax's eyes locked with mine once more. The corner of his mouth curved up. "The last time I took a girl on a date, I was still in the military. I might be a bit rusty."

My breath caught in my throat. I wondered if it was Alison.

Callie scoffed. "I'm not sure this should count as a date. Kidnapping, maybe. But definitely not a date." She leaned toward me. "Blink twice if you were kidnapped and need me to kill him."

It was kinda unnerving to feel like I fit in so easily. I hadn't ever felt as comfortable and accepted as I did in that truck.

If I'd known how my life would change just by working at Jacob and Lily's wedding, I wouldn't change a thing. I'd clumsily bump into Jax and fall like I just learned to walk. I'd still have taken his jacket. And I still would have said yes to our little date. Even though the date thing didn't really work out...

We might be moving fast and not what would be considered appropriate or normal for others, but it felt right.

Watching Flapjack and Callie and hearing the stories of how they were as a family gave me hope that love was real. It was possible. And if I said I was scared, that would be an understatement.

But I watched Jax's hand on my leg and then looked up at him, and I knew. I wanted to fall madly, deeply, and irrevocably in love with someone in such a way that they would drop everything to find me if I was in a plane crash or taken like Flapjack was or avenge and save me like all the girls they've rescued over the years. But I didn't want to love just anyone. I wanted Jax.

Should I be so concerned that I was growing attached so quickly? Possibly. But I wasn't in the mood to psychoanalyze myself. At this point, I could probably walk into any therapist's office, and they'd take one look at me and say, *"You have abandonment issues. PTSD. And depression. Take these pills."* As if the medicine would be some magic cure.

Although the first step would be admitting the things I lived through actually happened. Jax was the first person I ever told, and that was only a glimpse into my life. I wasn't going to try to figure out why I could tell him my secrets and not my best friend. I guess maybe I always assumed Dani knew the truth.

"I'm feeling much better. Thank you." I slid off his lap, hating to leave his comfort, but there was no reason for him to have dead legs by the time we reached wherever we were going.

I settled into my seat, wincing slightly as the seatbelt brushed over my bruised rib. I felt a lot better today, but the bruises would take a few more days. I was just grateful that's all I had to deal with. Even the cut on my hand ended up being superficial.

Flapjack's phone dinged. "Diesel said Jacob landed and is waiting for us at the private terminal outside the base."

The more they talked, the more I wondered if they were like the mafia. *A private terminal?*

I knew Jax said he wasn't in the mafia, but it was very suspicious. Not that I'd ever met anyone in the mafia to compare them to.

I smirked at myself. It was absurd for my first thought to go right to mobsters.

Jax grabbed my hand, pulling it to his leg. I grinned. He might not be in the mafia, but he was my beast.

Chapter 18

Jax

Past trauma can create unhealthy attachments. I'd seen enough of that at Ana's Place. The therapists we employed have expressed concern for me multiple times, saying I was *attached* to work and needed a new, healthy 'obsession.'

Rubbing small circles over Bryer's hand, I wasn't sure this was what they meant, but I wouldn't want to change it. Fuck being healthy. I was a fucked up mess and spent years trying to save others, hoping it would *fix* me. I thought if I could save the right person, it would make up for losing the others. But having Bryer next to me, feeling her pulse under my fingertips, resurfaced a part of the man I was before... the man who I thought died. I wasn't stuck in the revolving memory of being unable to save Alison because I was focused on protecting my angel.

Bryer was saving me.

And the therapists could go to hell if they thought I would give her up. Besides, she looked cute as fuck with that toothpick hanging from her mouth.

I squeezed her hand tighter, closed my eyes, and leaned my head back. Right now, I needed her more than ever. I was trying not to think about Bear, but it was impossible. If I could play rock, paper, scissors to get him out of this now, I would. And I'd make sure to let him win.

We made it to the airstrip between the airport and the military base. Jacob was already there with Lily. His forlorn, weary look told of a long night and the worry we all felt.

It brought back the seriousness of the situation. Bear was our brother, and he needed us.

We all climbed out of the trucks, and I retook Bryer's hand, pulling her close to my side as we walked.

Diesel gave Jacob a quick hug. "I'm glad you made it."

Sam took Lily into her arms. "With Flapjack leading the way at a hundred miles an hour, I'm surprised we didn't beat you here."

Jacob chuckled. "There is a reason why I let him drive."

"It was the fastest trip to Idaho I've ever taken." Fox yawned, stretching out his arms and back.

Diesel grunted. "That's because you slept through the whole thing."

Fox flipped Diesel off. For a moment, I could almost pretend that everything was okay and that we were just waiting for Bear. But he never showed.

We gathered in a circle, all waiting for any news we hoped Jacob had.

He looked over us all, landing on Bryer. "I wish we were meeting under better circumstances. If Jax brought you here, then I don't think I have to tell you you're already family. And in this family, we have rules. First rule, there are no solo missions. We do this together. In this family, we're all in. We never leave a man behind and have each other's back in all we do. If one of us finds trouble, we all find it. But we will have lots of time to talk after, when we *all* are home."

Bryer nodded in quiet agreement.

Jacob looked down with his eyes shut, cursing under his breath before lifting his head. "I'm not gonna lie, this doesn't look good. There hasn't been any communication from Bear or Wes since the moment the plane went down."

"Are you certain they crashed?" Callie folded her arms, looking to Jacob for the answers I also wanted.

He ran a hand over his face. "Yeah. There is nowhere for a plane to land where his coordinates are."

"So, you know where he's at?" Flapjack wrapped an arm around his wife's shoulders, and I couldn't tell who was supporting who.

Jacob cocked his head in a brief nod. "We know where his tracker is. And it hasn't moved in hours." He winced, looking away from us for a moment before continuing. "I'm not giving up, but I am preparing for the worst." He looked right at me. "I know you all care about Bear. We've all been through hell and back for each other multiple times, and I don't ever expect you to stop, but fuck…"

"Just come on out and say it." I had a feeling I already knew what was about to happen and was torn on how far I was willing to argue with Jacob.

He looked at Lily, who nodded for him to go ahead and just tell us. He released a quick breath. "Not everyone can go this time."

A collective murmur and a few shouts echoed through our group.

"Fuck that." Diesel huffed, and the man's shoulders tensed. "We always go together."

Jacob looked so much older and worn out right then. I knew this was weighing on him heavily. "Give us a reason," I urged.

He glanced at me with hope springing back in his eyes. "Where we're going, I could only find two helicopters, a search and rescue crew, and medical personnel. I don't know what Bear needs, but there is a high chance he's gonna need a doctor before he needs a brother. I'm not willing to risk losing him over a few hours to keep us all happy." He shook his head. "Damn it. This is not what I want either. While I would want any one of you to be the ones to come after me in the heart of the fucking Ring down in Mexico, the side of the mountain, repelling, and God only knows what else we might encounter, this is not our specialty."

"Oh, shit! Oh, shit! Fuck." Fox sputtered a few more curses, holding up his phone.

There wasn't an eye on him while he freaked out. If *he* was cursing… it was bad.

"It's Bear! He called me… or tried… or something. Shit, I don't know. I was sleeping!"

My heart plummeted. "Why the fuck would he call you?"

"Give me that!" Diesel yanked Fox's phone from his hands. "Damn it! What the fuck, Fox? He could have been… What if…"

Not even Diesel could finish that sentence.

Fox's eyes rimmed with tears. "I didn't know. I didn't hear it. I'm sorry."

"Sorry doesn't cut it this time, kid." Flapjack glowered at Fox. "If that was his last—"

"Don't fucking say it," I interrupted.

If looks could kill, Fox would have been massacred. There wasn't a single one of us who wasn't shooting daggers at him.

Jacob bit his tongue and grimaced, shaking his head as he stared at Fox's cell. "Everyone, call Bear. Text him. Don't stop trying. If there's a chance we can get a message to him, make it count."

He didn't have to elaborate on what *make it count* meant. It hung heavily in the air. The implication that it might be the last thing Bear sees was important.

Fox took his phone and began typing furiously on the screen. He stared at it as if willing Bear to call back.

"Lily is staying behind as well." Jacob looked at her. "I don't think I have to say this to anyone, but I'm trusting whoever stays with my wife's life."

My gut twisted. I knew Bryer wouldn't be one that should go either, but I wasn't ready to let anyone else be her protector. And with her bruises from her fall a few days ago, strenuous hiking, lifting, or repelling wouldn't be easy for her. I knew she would do it. It was in her nature to obey and quietly go along with the pain, but fuck that. I was going to teach her it was okay to not be okay. "I'll stay."

Those two words had everyone staring at me. "You can't." Diesel paled. "You're our best tracker. You can't just leave Bear up there. I'll stay."

Jacob shook his head. "No, I need you. You have experience rock climbing and spent last summer with the underground search and rescue."

Diesel cursed. "That's for underground, not on a fucking mountain. Jax is way more qualified. He can find anything!"

Jacob paused, grinding his jaw. "But we know where Bear is. Finding him isn't the hard part."

Flapjack glanced at Callie. "I'll do it. I'll stay."

Sam folded her arms and shook her head. "That's ridiculous. You're the only one who might be able to forage food and keep them *all* alive."

Callie pursed her lips together before speaking. "Jax, I know your head isn't in the right place. A lot has changed in the last twenty-four hours. I agree. It might be best for you to stay."

I wasn't sure if I was gutted that she pointed that out in front of everyone or relieved I had someone on my side.

Jacob nodded at me. "Alright. It's decided. I hate to agree, but Callie is right. From what I'm hearing, your mindset is elsewhere." He put a hand on my shoulder. "Fill me in when we get back, alright? For now, take Fox with you. I'll deal with him later."

Fox swallowed hard and visibly shrank.

Callie stepped forward. "I'll stay too. I'm great with a gun, but if..." She shook her head and fought to collect her breathing *and* her thoughts. "But if things are not like we hope, I'm not sure I can do it. I don't want to be in the way."

Jacob's shoulders pulled back as he looked at the rest of them directly. "I need one more to stay. There's only room for three of us with the flight crews, paramedics, and search and rescue team."

"It's only right that I stay." Sam looked at Diesel. "He needs you guys."

Diesel touched her face and nodded.

"We leave in fifteen minutes." Jacob took Lily's hand and walked with her to the trucks. "Jax, you good with the lead?"

I nodded.

"Sam, you follow him back to the ranch. Stay together." Jacob helped his wife in the passenger seat and kissed her.

Diesel followed suit, holding Sam close before making sure she was settled in the driver's seat.

Fox looked lost before climbing in behind them. Smart man. Being in my truck right now wouldn't be wise. I didn't want to look at him right now. Brother or not, I was pissed.

How could he sleep through something so important?

I opened the door for Bryer and helped her into the truck. Callie got in behind her. No one was talking. Leaving Idaho without Bear was not something I had planned on or wanted. It gutted me to get into the driver's seat and be the one to drive away.

In forty years, I'd never had to question my instincts. I wasn't about to start now. I made the decision to leave because Bryer needed me. I was the best tracker, but they had Flapjack. He would find Bear.

Placing the truck in drive felt wrong. We rarely separated on a hunt. No solo missions.

But this wasn't a hunt, and my mission was to keep the girls safe. Fox was about to grow the fuck up because I wasn't going to let him sleep for a week.

The ranch had a beautiful layer of snow covering the ground. It took us longer to get back than it did to get out. The winter was going to be a hard one this year.

"Can I borrow your phone?" Bryer asked as we drove up the long, windy road.

"Always." I forgot hers was shattered in pieces on a floor in town. I handed her my cell.

She swiped it open and smiled. "That's me."

I looked over. I'd taken the picture covertly at the wedding. I gave half a chuckle. "Yeah."

Her smile widened. "That's sweet."

Callie made swoony noises. "Big brother has a girlfriend."

I glared at her in the rearview mirror. "Are you in fucking kindergarten?"

She laughed. "No, but I am trying to distract myself from my thoughts, and guess what... bugging you seems to be the winner."

Fucking great.

Bryer punched in a number and waited on the line. She frowned when it went to voicemail. She tried a different number. Her brow furrowed. "It's not like Dani to not pick up. Or Alice." She handed me my phone.

"Tell you what, after the others get settled in, we'll head to town. You need a new phone, and then we can check on your friends."

"Really? I don't want you to go out of your way for me. Besides, Bear—"

"Bear," I interjected. "Will be okay. And we'll be home before he is. I have my phone if anything happens, and they can get ahold of me. Right, Callie?" I looked in the mirror, pointedly giving her *the look*.

"You have to take her to dinner too." She smirked, folding her arms and leaning back in her seat. "Word of advice. If you get frisky, lock the bathroom doors."

Dear Lord. I didn't want to have the image in my head of fucking Bryer in a public bathroom. Mine, absolutely. Someplace where someone has pissed all over the floor? Fuck no.

Bryer blushed. "Dinner sounds nice."

Going out, eating, town... it all sounded so mundane compared to whatever Bear might be going through. It was easy to see why some people felt guilty when a loved one was sick, injured, or even dead to continue living as if nothing was wrong.

But that was the whole point. I was alive. Bryer was alive. We don't stop existing when someone stops breathing. It might feel like it, but we don't.

Bear would come home pissed if he heard I stopped living my life because of him. I could imagine the man yelling now, and I almost smiled.

Callie was right. A distraction from the present was the only way we would get through this. And while Bryer was so much more than that, I could think of a few ways to bide our time.

Chapter 19

Bryer

Walking into Jax's room, I instantly felt my skin flush as I remembered last night. He set our bags on the bed.

Giving one of my bags a pat, he looked at me. "Don't unpack this one, just in case."

If we had to leave quickly again, we would be prepared. It made sense.

I strolled around the room and noticed a painting leaning against the wall behind another bag. I squatted to look at it. The darkness beckoned me, and while it was stupid, the rose in the middle almost made me cry. I felt entirely too emotional. Touching the painting, the piece spoke to me. It was familiar. Like the artist pulled what I felt and thought out of me and put it on the canvas.

"It's beautiful, isn't it." Jax touched my shoulder.

"It's perfect." I stood, still looking down at the rose.

"It made me think of you." He picked it up and set it on the dresser so we could admire it openly.

I leaned into him. "It's like whoever painted it is inside my head."

He kissed my cheek. "Well, someday, you can ask her all about it."

I cocked my head. "How?"

"She is one of the girls who live at our safe house in Texas. Her name is Isabelle."

"You rescued her?"

He nodded. "She was one of the girls on the island where Flapjack was taken."

Oh my goodness. I clutched at my chest. There was so much pain in the painting, and now I understood.

"Are you sure you want to go to town?"

He nodded. "We won't hear anything for a while. Sitting here won't make them find Bear any faster."

"Is it okay if I get cleaned up a bit? I'd love a shower first."

Heat pooled in his eyes as he stared at me. "Of course. It's your home too. Do whatever you want. You don't have to ask me for permission."

It didn't feel like mine. But I wasn't about to argue with him about it right now. He was going through enough.

He picked up my larger suitcase and put it on the bed. "You can unpack this one, though." He winked.

God help me. That look went straight between my legs.

He tapped the luggage as if contemplating everything. "I know I told you that you can use the spare room, but—"

I stepped forward, touching his chest. "If you're ok, I meant what I said about staying in your room."

He wrapped his arms around me, resting his head on mine. "*Our* room."

I melted into him, breathing him in and burning this moment into my memories. One by one, I had a feeling he would fight the demons in my head like the beast he was. Each second I spent with him pushed out my fear, giving me a strange but peaceful feeling of comfort that I craved.

Pulling back, I twisted to remove myself from his hold and unzipped the suitcase, looking for fresh clothes. Finding what I needed, I held them to me and turned to find Jax watching me with a hungry stare.

"I'll be just a minute." Ducking my head, I slipped out of the room and into the bathroom.

There were towels on the shelves where I set my clothes. Undressing, I took a minute to look in the mirror. The bruises were looking much better. However, green and brown were not my favorite colors.

I ran my hands over my breasts down to my stomach, where I stopped. The extra bit hung lower, and I tried to cover it up. I couldn't believe I let Jax see me naked. He must be so disgusted and repulsed by what we'd done.

Tears sprang to my eyes. I've never cared how much I weighed or how I looked to someone else, but I wished I had. For the first time in my life, I wanted to be beautiful.

The way Jax looked at me made me feel like no one was sexier than me. That I was Aphrodite in the flesh. But my heart twinged and twisted because I knew that wasn't true.

Turning to the side didn't make me feel any better about myself. I was only twenty-two, but my boobs weren't as perky as other girls and barely a handful. Having a C cup, I was average. But to be fair, I wished they made B-and-a-half cups because that would fit better.

My hips were too straight, and my legs were usually swollen from being on my feet all day. I slipped my contacts out, not wanting to see any more.

It didn't matter how much I tried. I would never be the Beast's Beauty.

A slight rap of knuckles on the door made me jump.

"Bryer? You okay?"

I sucked in a shaky breath. "Yeah. Why?"

"I thought I heard something and came to make sure everything was okay, but then I noticed the water wasn't on. You're not in there hiding from me… are you?" The lilt and humor in his tone made me smile.

I cocked my head toward the door to listen for him. "Why, sir, are you listening outside the door?"

"Maybe."

I smirked. "Pervert."

"Correction. Overprotective beast who has a queen to look after."

My heart thundered in my chest. "I'm surprised you didn't break the door down."

"Is that an invitation?"

My clit tingled at his response. "I'm getting in the shower."

I turned the water on and waited for it to get hot before stepping inside. I pulled the shower curtain back a smidgen. "No reason to stand there like a guard."

The door opened, and I squealed, shutting the curtain.

"Sorry," he laughed. "I couldn't hear you from out there. I guess I'll have to join you."

He wouldn't.

The curtain pulled back.

He would.

I blinked and tried to cover myself.

He removed my hands and pressed me up against the wall. "A little late, little wolf. I've already seen everything about you. And you are most desirable."

My mouth dried. He pressed into me, his cock hardening against my leg. His mouth found mine in a savage kiss.

"Damn, it's hot." He chuckled and turned the dial slightly, but not enough to completely freeze me out.

I was so lost in his kiss and how his body was pressed against mine to care about the water.

He grabbed a bottle of body wash and poured it on his palm. "Turn around."

Wait. What? I was so lost. First, he was kissing me, but now he wants to just wash me? I was so flushed and needing more than a shower now.

He leaned in, the water spraying us both. "I won't ask twice, angel."

I bit my bottom lip and contemplated disobeying him. I reached out, gripping his hard cock, not breaking his stare.

The hunger in his eyes deepened. "My defiant little wolf."

I stepped closer so the tip of his length touched my stomach. "My demanding beast."

I stroked him.

He growled. "You are playing with fire."

His cock pulsed as I reached the base. He was so big my fingers couldn't touch. "I believe I'm playing with something *much* harder."

The deep guttural groan that vibrated in his chest had me on the brink of an orgasm, and he wasn't even touching me. It was crazy how turned on this man made me. Going from practically hating all men to being obsessed with one was strange but beautiful. I never imagined I would see the day that I'd be standing in a shower, giving my heart to a vigilante while I stroked his cock.

Jax gripped both of my wrists, making me stop. He lifted my hands above my head, holding them against the wall, and smirked. "Baby girl, you are going to take everything I give you."

My chest heaved, and my nipples barely grazed him, creating a hot, tingling sensation along my skin. "On one condition."

He nibbled at my lips. "I'll do anything you want, angel."

"Don't hurt me." My words were barely a whisper. I was so scared. This was uncharted territory for me, and while my body was clearly ready for it, my mind was spinning out of control.

His head snapped up, and his fierce gaze locked with mine. "Never."

I knew he meant it. Everything I was; my heart, body, and soul was safe with him. This man was a gift I didn't intend on ever letting go.

His mouth was on mine in a savage caress. He wasn't just kissing me. It felt like he was doing more... branding my soul with his name and claiming my body as his. I was lost to Jax Harper. Not even my thoughts belonged to me anymore.

The way his grip on my wrists tightened excited me. He pressed into me, his cock pulsed against my stomach, but I wanted to feel it in *other* places. "Jax, please."

My voice was raspy and sounded so far away I wondered if I'd actually spoken.

"My little wolf is impatient. But you disobeyed me, so now you must take your punishment."

My heart skipped a beat, and I closed my eyes. I didn't think his kind of punishment was the same as what I was used to, but it scared me a little. I moved my head, breaking the kiss.

His free hand gently gripped my chin, turning me back to face him. "Bryer, look at me."

I looked up at him, trying not to panic. The hot water created steam around us and reminded me that I was in the shower. Naked. With Jax.

"I will never hurt you." He returned to pecking light kisses along my jaw. "But you didn't listen when I asked you to turn around. Baby girl, your punishment will be me dragging this out."

I was so confused. *That* was his punishment? "But I thought you wanted me?"

He pressed his cock harder into my stomach. "I think you can feel how much I want you. Don't ever doubt that."

"I'm not like other girls. I'm flabby and imperfect. I can't even see you clearly right now. My thighs touch—"

He growled. "Fuck me. Angel, you are the most beautiful woman I've ever seen. And your fucking thighs are exquisite. I can't wait to die between them. And if you ever talk down about this perfect body again, I will have to draw out an orgasm that lasts until you know you are a goddess. My beauty."

Holy. Fucking. Shit.

My heart beat so fast, I was sure it would crash and burn, leaving me to die writhing in Jax's arms.

He pulled back. "You can't see me?"

"A little. I mean, I can see you, but not all your details."

He scooped me up and shut the water off.

"What are you doing?" I squealed with a short laugh.

"Making sure you can see who is giving you pleasure."

I blushed and tried to wiggle from his arms. I was too big for him to be carrying around, but apparently, he was stronger than I thought because he didn't even let me slip a little.

In the room, he placed me on the bed. "I'm assuming you have contacts."

I nodded. "In there, with my glasses." I pointed to the luggage Dani packed for me.

He rummaged around until he pulled out my glasses and came to the bed, slipping them on my face.

I ducked, attempting to take them off.

He gripped my hand. "Leave them on."

"Jax, I look—"

"Absolutely stunning." He smirked. "Now, when you scream my name, I want your eyes open on me."

God help me. If he kept talking like that, I was going to die. I never blinked as I nodded.

"Good girl." He kneeled and grabbed my knees. He spread me open without breaking my stare. His hands traveled up my legs to my thighs, where he gripped the flesh and groaned. "Fuck, baby girl." He leaned in, kissing every place his fingers touched.

The slow burn, slithering toward my center, was agonizing. I was so wet I was practically dripping onto the bed.

His lips worked their way deliberately up the inside of my thighs. He was so close.

I gripped the bedding and lifted my hips, wanting to guide him to the one place I needed to feel him. He growled and grabbed my hips, holding me to the bed. "I told you, little wolf, you have to take your punishment."

I cried out, needing to find a release from the build-up he was creating. This was the most exquisite form of punishment, but I wondered how I would survive it.

His finger swiped up through my slit. The soft pressure was a shock, but I craved more. He leaned back and locked eyes with me once more, bringing his finger to his mouth, and sucked me off him. He closed his eyes and hung his head back. "Fuck, you taste so good." The way his mouth curved was devilish. He reached over and grabbed a toothpick from the nightstand.

I watched. No way he was going to do what I thought he was...

He twirled the smooth edge of the small pick over my opening, coating it in my wetness before setting it down. It was hard not to notice how soaked it was.

The sound that escaped my throat was equally dangerous. The dark, feral look in his eyes deepened, and he dove in, capturing my clit in his mouth.

I fell back on the bed, sure I would die. I was wound so tightly that I was ready to explode. I thread my fingers through his hair, gripping his head as he licked my opening. His hands were under me, lifting my ass to give him better access.

Every muscle in me tightened, and I was so close to falling over the precipice into pleasure.

Jax pulled away. An evil glint in his stare was followed by a wink. He wiped his mouth, licking his lips like a wild animal that had just devoured their dinner.

"Jax," I whispered. I was so close. Reaching down, I pressed a finger to my clit.

His hand quickly went around my wrist. "Don't even think about it, angel."

God, this *was* punishment. I locked eyes with him and knew he had only begun. He removed my hand and thrust a finger inside of me.

I cried out and was quickly greeted with a second finger, but he left, leaving me inching to the edge of the bed, wanting him to come back.

When he didn't, I raised up on my elbows and watched as he wrapped his fingers, coated in my wetness, around his cock. I stopped breathing.

His eyes were on me. "Do you want to touch me?"

Fuck, I wanted to touch him, stroke him, take him inside of me. I nodded. I couldn't form words, but I was eager to give him everything he was giving me.

He pushed me back and climbed on top of me, straddling my chest. He was careful of my ribs, but hell, I didn't care if he squeezed me as long as I could die with him inside of me.

He was so close I could easily grip him with both hands and wasn't about to let that gift go. I took him in my hands, slowly stroking him from the base to the tip that dripped precum.

He tipped his head back and groaned. "Fuck."

I smirked because I was only beginning. Cupping his balls, I gently caressed the soft, sensitive spot in the middle. His cock jerked in my other hand. I grinned, knowing I hit the right place.

Jax pulled back and picked me up, placing me in the center of the bed. He crawled over me and returned to his position. I wondered why he moved us until he leaned forward, grasping the headboard.

This man... seeing his muscles tighten had me so wet I felt it pooling under me. I needed him in any way I could get him. Gripping his ass with one hand, I urged him forward, opening my mouth. I didn't stop stroking him and twirled my tongue over the tip. He was dripping precum, and I wanted to taste it all.

He was so big, I worried I wouldn't be able to fit him in my mouth, let alone my pussy, but I was past caring if I choked on him. There was at least two hundred pounds of muscle hovering over me, like the beast he was, letting me lead him.

I tried to guide him into my mouth, but he pulled back. I swear to God, if he denied me this, I would shatter into the depths of hell.

He stared down at me, looking every bit of the monster he said he was, but I knew he would fight every demon who came my way. I never felt worthy of such a protector, but damn if he didn't make me feel like I was a queen.

"You want to suck me down that pretty little throat?" His voice was low and breathy.

I nodded and opened my mouth again.

He thrust into me but was being too careful, not going as far as I wanted. I sucked and grabbed his ass, pulling him down, forcing him deeper into my throat.

"Fuck. Bryer."

I dug my fingers into his flesh, and he obeyed my directions, choking me with his cock. The headboard cracked and groaned as he held on. Thrusting into me, his balls tightened, and I knew he was close.

I moaned, loving how I could bring him to this point. His length filled my throat, preventing me from breathing. I gagged and felt the hot tears stream from my eyes in a blissful display of agonizing pleasure.

"Fuck, angel, I'm gonna come. Can you take me like a good girl?"

I nodded. I wanted him to come and sucked harder. I felt the stream of cum hit the back of my throat at the same time as Jax moaned my name. His cock pulsed in my mouth, and I licked him from the base to the tip, swallowing every last drop he offered.

His growl echoed in the room as he climbed off and flipped us so I was now straddling him. His length still twitched under my clit, making me very aware of just how aroused I was.

"I think my angel is done with her punishment." He grasped the back of my head and pulled me down to him, capturing my mouth. "I don't know what the fuck that was, but I'm beginning to think my angel has a dark side. I haven't ever come that fast before."

He sucked on my tongue, and I knew he could taste himself, and I almost came right then. Why was that such a turn on?

He licked his lips and rubbed them together. "Now let me taste you before I fuck you."

I cocked my head. I was not prepared to hear him say that. After sucking him down, I didn't think he'd be able to do more. I wasn't complaining, but I was lying to myself if I said I wasn't excited about the prospect of making him come more than once today.

"I said I want my dessert, little wolf."

"I'm not sure how from this angle."

He gripped my hips and lifted me, setting me on his face. I squealed and tried to get off him. "I can't do that!"

"You can and you will. Sit the fuck down and let me taste you."

I hesitated, barely hovering over him. He would suffocate if I sat on him.

"I don't ask twice, baby girl."

Shit.

"You're dripping wet. Fuck." His tongue was hot as he slid it inside of me.

He pulled me down, and I cried out as he filled me. He groaned and feasted on my pussy, teasing my clit and licking me senseless. I couldn't think. I could only react. I grabbed the headboard and hoped I wouldn't fall.

I felt myself diving over the edge before I exploded. I sank into his mouth and cried out.

He moved out from under me and flipped me onto my back. Grabbing behind my knees, he pushed them up toward my chest and pressed his cock at my entrance.

"I need to hear you say it, Bryer."

"Yes. Please." I was breathless and slightly dizzy but wanted more. Already, I could feel my nerves tightening.

"I'll go slow." He broke through the entrance, and I braced myself for the sting I remembered from years ago, but it was a much different pain.

I stretched almost painfully thin to fit him. I wiggled, looking for some space between us, and tensed. Maybe I couldn't do this after all.

"Shhh," he cooed in my ear. "I've got you. You're safe. You're taking me so well. Fuck." He groaned.

Hearing him praise me had me relaxing. He was so big, I wasn't sure if I could take all of him. I was close to using my safe word. Fear began to override the excitement.

He reached down and stroked my clit. "You need to relax, angel. You're so fucking tight."

His fingers were like magic as he caressed me. I raised my hips, feeling him inside me when I tightened up. Damn, he was moving deeper.

"A little more." His husky whisper had me wanting to take all of him.

I wound my arms around his neck and pulled him to me. "Give it to me. All of it."

He pushed in all the way, burying deep inside me.

I cried out and clawed at his shoulders. "Holy shit."

He waited for a minute before slowly pulling out and then thrusting back inside.

"You were made for me, baby girl." He plunged into the depths of my pussy.

I tightened around him and felt so full. He was so far inside me that I wasn't sure where he began and where I ended. I felt him in my soul.

He ravaged my body, kissing and touching me everywhere. His hand caressed my breast, rubbing and pinching my nipples.

He lifted my hips and thrust his cock, hitting a spot that had my vision disappearing. "Jax!"

"Louder." He rammed into me. "Scream for me."

Wild and almost desperately, he filled me. He was panting and groaning.

I stopped breathing and stilled as the most intense feeling captured me, holding me hostage... and the only man who could save me was Jax.

"Look at me, angel. I want to see my beauty fall apart as I come inside her."

Fuck!

I focused on him, but it was spotty and fading fast. "Jax," I whispered.

The darkness that held me was the same thing that killed me. My soul exploded, leaving my body.

I screamed for Jax until my throat was raw, leaving me to whimper and writhe under him as he thrust into me one last time. He stiffened, holding himself over me as his cock pulsed inside me. I could feel his cum filling me so full I would be feeling him for days.

He kissed my forehead and slowly pulled out of me. "Stay right here."

It was such a lonely, disappointing feeling to have him leave so quickly after, but he slipped out of the room and was back again so soon that it was a fleeting emotion.

He took a warm, wet cloth and began cleaning me up, wiping through the most sensitive part of me. I couldn't help but moan as he passed over my clit.

He rubbed over it again without the cloth. "I can't stop with you. You're like a drug." He pressed harder and circled it. "I want to watch you come."

Isn't that what he just did? It was so soon, I was already close. I lifted my hips, widening my legs.

"That's my girl." He sat on his knees and watched my pussy as he played with me.

I tightened but didn't hold onto it this time and let it take me over. I fell apart with his hand cupping me. Glasses or not, I had a hard time seeing anything and reached for him.

He licked the palm of his hand. "Such a good girl."

How soon was too soon to know someone was meant to be yours? Because, at that moment, time wasn't a factor. I had never considered myself a possessive type of girl, but Jax was mine.

Chapter 20

Jax

I wanted to spend the rest of the day tangled in the sheets with Bryer, but I told her we could go to town. I wanted her to know I always kept my word and meant what I said. To give her some semblance of stability in someone she could rely on.

Besides, getting away from the ranch might make waiting for news of Bear easier. Each minute that passed without a phone call from Jacob killed me a little on the inside.

Focusing on Bryer was lifesaving.

"I promise. Alice and I will probably just sit around talking about you. We can lock the doors and everything." She was trying hard to let me drop her off at her friend's house while I went to get her a new phone.

"Fine." I wasn't a dictator. I just wanted her safe.

She grinned victoriously.

Pulling up to Alice's house, Bryer sat in the passenger seat and waited for me to come around and open it for her. I scanned the area but didn't see a threat. Not that I believed I would.

I opened the door and helped her out. "You are getting rewarded for waiting for me later tonight."

I twirled the toothpick that still tasted like her over my tongue.

I loved the dark blush that crested her cheeks. I walked her up to the door. Alice answered with a bubbly smile, pulling Bryer in for a hug. "I'm so glad you're here!"

"I'll be back soon, okay?" I tipped Bryer's chin and removed my toothpick so I could give her a kiss. Making sure she could taste herself on my tongue wasn't helping the raging hard-on I had.

Damn, she was like the air I breathed. I was falling quickly, and my heart skipped a few beats. Looking over at Alice, I added, "Keep her safe. You have my number. Call me if Rick or anyone else shows up."

"Trust me, they have to go through me to get to her. Have you seen a pissed-off redhead?"

I chuckled and shook my head. "I don't envy anyone who makes you mad."

Bryer took my hand. I could feel her heart racing in her wrist.

"Don't worry, angel, I'll be right back. Go enjoy your time with Alice." I winked at her. "Don't tell her any lies about me though."

She rolled her eyes, and I walked away, letting her hand slide from mine. Closing the door, I could already hear Alice asking her all about her night at the ranch. I shook my head and jumped into the truck.

It took over an hour to pick out a new phone and activate it for Bryer. It was the latest android with all the bells and whistles. She deserved the best. I would rather go back to payphones than use an iOS system.

Her side of the truck was empty, and I knew I wouldn't last long without going back for her. But giving her time without me was healthy. We had already moved so fast. It was strange to think it had only been a few days.

The sun was already kissing the horizon. The shorter days were hard for some, but I kind of enjoyed them. The things we could do in the dark made my heart skip a beat.

The toothpick still tasted like her, and I savored it. Pushing down on my cock, I knew the hard-on wasn't going anywhere for a while. I wonder if Bryer would be up for christening the back seats of the cab.

Or maybe holding onto the tailgate, bent over, and taking me from behind.

I sucked on the toothpick and groaned.

Driving through town, it was hard not to speed. I glanced at my watch. Almost two hours since I dropped her off.

Pulling up to Alice's house, I knew something was wrong. The front door was open, and inside, a chair was tipped over. I grabbed my gun from the glovebox and jumped from the truck, racing up the walk.

I pushed inside. "Bryer!" Taking in the scene, I needed to slow down and concentrate.

Fuck. Where was she?

"Alice?"

I spun, pointing the gun directly at Dani's chest. He stopped in the doorway and held his hands up. "Whoa. Don't shoot."

"What the fuck happened? Where's Bryer?"

Dani's brow furrowed. "Bryer? What are you talking about? You lost her? Where's Alice?"

"Check outside for anyone. Everywhere. Cars, sheds, bushes… don't leave a fucking leaf unturned." I started for the back of the house, not waiting to make sure Dani could follow an order. Both rooms looked untouched; nothing was out of place, beds were made, and clothes hung in the master room closet.

Son of a bitch.

Returning to the front room, Dani came back into the house. I raised my gun in his direction. "You just conveniently popped in at the same time?"

He raised his hands. "What are you talking about?"

"Where is she? I'm not lowering this until you tell me what's going on."

"Fuck, man. I don't know. I told Alice I'd come over after work." His eyes went past me to the room, and his face paled. "What the fuck?"

I lowered the gun and stuck it in the waist of my jeans. "Listen to me. I need you to do exactly as I say."

He stared at the scene but nodded.

"I need you to focus. The girls are gone, but we're gonna find them." And whoever took them was going to die. I wouldn't even waste time with torture. I would be the judge and executioner with one swift bullet.

Alison's face flashed in my mind but was quickly replaced with Bryer's. It was Bryer being raped and abused. It was her lifeless body I cradled.

I clenched the toothpick between my teeth. "Go talk to the neighbors, see if they saw anything. I'm going to look for clues."

Dani hesitated.

"Go!"

He took off, leaving me alone in the room. I studied the mess. A streak of blood was smeared into the carpet. It wasn't much. At least there wasn't blood spray. It gave me hope that whoever was bleeding wasn't hurt seriously. It wasn't a gunshot.

Dani came running back. "One of them saw a black car but nothing more."

People often looked the other way, not wanting to become part of the problem themselves. It infuriated me that so many had such self-preservation that kept them from helping those in need. And it was the innocent who died.

I twirled the toothpick and scanned the rest of the area. "Do you know anyone with a black car? Someone that might know Bryer or Alice?"

"No." He looked lost. I was reminded that not everyone could handle this part of life. It was the part the media hid from the public.

"Hey, stay with me. The girls need you to stay focused. If you lose it now, they could get hurt." Or worse. But I wasn't about to send him into a spiraling panic.

He nodded. "What can I do?"

"I need you to go to Bryer's apartment and see if anything has been moved. See if anyone besides us has been there. You were there last, so you'll know more than I would."

"Yeah. Alright. Then what?"

"Then we start going door to fucking door if we have to." I needed to call Sam. She could help and have an inside thought process. After being the hitman for a notorious sex trafficker, she knew how they worked and where they might have gone.

I wasn't sure what happened, but I wouldn't waste time thinking small. It wasn't in my nature. If I jumped right to kidnapping and trafficking, then I could help Bryer faster.

Dani left, and I grabbed my phone, dialing Sam.

She answered on the second ring. "If you're calling for sex advice, you should just buy a book with pictures. They have those, you know."

I felt my heart sink. "She's gone. Bryer... Fuck, Sam. I need you."

"What? Where are you?"

I told her what happened and worried I was wasting too much time rehashing everything, but I knew I needed to talk it out with someone. No solo missions.

"Shit. Okay. We're on our way."

I could hear Lily in the background, "Damn, this family doesn't do anything small."

I almost chuckled. She wasn't wrong. "Thank you."

I hung up, and my phone rang. It was Dani. "What'd you find?"

"It's not a mess, but I heard Rick say her name... he's down in the main house, and he's beating the shit out of Bryer's mom."

"Get the fuck down there and stop him!" Damn. That kid was going to test my patience. I ran to the truck.

Getting to the apartment, I barely had the truck in park before jumping out. There was shouting coming from the main house. I pulled my gun out and opened the door.

Dani had Rick in a chokehold, but it wasn't strong enough to bring the man down. But he had gotten Rick to stop beating his wife. I had to give the kid some props.

I raised the gun. "Let him go, Dani."

Dani let go and ran over to a woman who lay unconscious on the floor. "She okay?"

He checked her pulse and nodded.

I kept my barrel trained on Rick. "You are a pathetic piece of shit. Does hurting a woman make you hard? Is that the only way you can get off?"

"Fuck you."

I pressed the gun to his forehead. "Big words for a fucking asshole who beats his wife and pimps his stepdaughter out."

Dani's head shot up, her wide eyes locked on me. "What?"

"Yeah. I know it all." Smiling at Rick, I cocked my head. "How about you and I take a walk."

"I'm not going anywhere with you." He squared his shoulders and glared at me.

"Oh, but you are. You see, I think you have something to do with Bryer missing. And I'm never wrong. I have this sixth sense. It's why I'm so good at what I do."

Rick scoffed. "You mean being a security guard?"

I leaned in. "No. I hunt bastards like you for a living, but I torture them for fun."

He paled. I pushed the gun harder to his head. "Turn around and start walking. Show me your basement."

His eyes widened. "I don't have one."

"Don't lie to me, Rick. I am very observant. And I don't ask twice."

"Alright! Fine." He held his hands up and walked to the door leading downstairs. I gave Dani a short nod. "I have some family headed this way. Let them in when they get here. Help Bryer's mom and stay out of the basement."

I knew Sam would use the tracker to find me. There was no doubt about it, when this was over, Bryer would have one as well. But right now, Rick and I were overdue for a *talk*.

Downstairs was unfinished, with drywall visible and wires going to lights. There was a poker table, cushioned folding chairs, a makeshift bar, and a few nude portraits of women hanging on the far wall. I didn't have to ask to know this was Rick's personal space. It was a sort of man cave, I guess. And it was a poor attempt at it, but it reeked of asshole.

I grabbed a chair and pulled it from the table. "Sit."

I scanned the room. There was a mess of housing materials in the corner. A slight grin lifted the corner of my mouth. Perfect.

Keeping the gun trained on him, I grabbed the box and pulled it over to the table, dumping it on the green felt.

"What the hell? You'll get grease all over my table." Rick stood up and attempted to come my way, but I held the gun up, gesturing to the chair.

"I told you. I don't ask twice." I shot him in the foot, making him fall into his seat with a yell.

"Fucker!" He cradled his foot, holding it up despite his portly beer belly and rocking. "Shit. You shot me!"

I grinned, not bothering to look back at him. "And I'm about to do worse things to you. Trust me, you'll be begging me to shoot you soon."

His foot was the least of his concerns. I ignored his whimpering and went back to work. I only wanted him to talk about one thing... Bryer.

Sifting through the mess, I pulled out a roll of wire and some cutters. Oh, this could be fun. There was enough to tie Rick up and still have fun.

I grabbed his wrists, brought them behind him, and tied the wire around them. Rick twisted and tried to get free, but I wasn't some fucking boy scout barely learning knots. I have done this for the fucking SEALS. I've held motherfuckers worse than him in harsher areas. No way was he getting loose.

"Now," I started while tying his legs. He kicked out, but it only made me chuckle. He was too slow and uncoordinated. He probably had enough alcohol in him to impair him, but adrenaline was about to wake him the fuck up.

"Tell me, Rick. Where's Bryer?"

"I don't fucking know. She's not here. How am I supposed to know?" He sneered up at me.

He won't be acting so tough in a minute. "I think you're lying to me." I squatted behind him. "Do you know what I do to liars?"

"You won't do shit. Let me go, and let's talk. I'm sure we can figure out where she's at," he snapped.

"Wrong answer." I yanked his hand up, loving how he shrieked when the cold metal of the wire clippers touched his skin. I clamped down on the handle. The tip of his pinky fell to the floor. I tsked, "I really don't like asking more than once."

Rick's screams ripped through the house. The door to the basement opened, and Dani called down. "Everything okay?"

I walked around Rick. "Shut the door, Dani."

"Shit. Someone's here." He closed the door.

Rick was close to hyperventilating. I slapped his face. "Hey, look up here, asshole. You don't get to panic and drown me out."

"You started without me?" Callie jogged down the stairs.

I should have known she would be the first one to volunteer to come to interrogate with me. Lily was the nurturer and would help Bryer's mom, while Sam guarded us all. I didn't have to give them orders. We were a family and had each other's backs. We knew where everyone would be and what they were doing. I relaxed, knowing they were there with me.

"He knows something." I couldn't explain how I knew things. It was like a gift of discernment. I just *knew*.

She eyed Rick. "Is this the piece of shit who beat that woman upstairs to a bloody pulp?"

"Yeah. He's also used his stepdaughter in ways I won't mention." I winced and tried to imagine younger Bryer, scared but so strong for handling everything thrown her way. "It's Bryer's stepdad."

"Vaffanculo." She was more Italian than Carter at times. Every time I heard her curse like that, I knew something was about to happen. She kneeled, looking up at him with an evil sneer. "You're not so big and bad now, are you. Fuckwad."

She pulled out a knife and looked over her shoulder at me. "Do you mind if I help?"

"We can take turns, but I want the last one."

She gave me a curt nod. "Understandable."

Being a mafia princess, this kind of stuff was right up her alley. While she was nothing like her father, she had an edge about her that made her seem crazy to anyone who didn't know her. Still, she was the one sister I knew would smile while walking through the fires of hell for any one of us.

She slipped the knife through Rick's pants until his thigh was exposed. "Have you ever seen an animal skinned?"

Rick swallowed hard and watched her knife. "What are you doing?"

She placed the blade to his leg. "Where's Bryer?"

His chest heaved. "Fuck you all. She's gone, and you aren't getting her back!"

Callie pulled the knife along his thigh, skinning him in a chunk to his knee. He screamed, and his head lolled to the side. What a lightweight. I'd tortured men who could hold out a lot longer, but apparently, Rick didn't have a high pain tolerance. Pity.

Callie dropped the skinned chunk to the floor and wiped her blade on his pants. "I feel so disappointed."

"I didn't want him passed out. I wanted him to talk."

"He'll wake up soon."

Just as she said it, Rick roused, moving his head back and forth, trying to remember what was happening. I grinned. "We're still here."

"Fuck."

"Tell me, Rick. Tell me what happened to her, and I'll make this quick and painless." I sifted through the mess on the table and found a pair of pliers. This box really was a gift that kept on giving.

His body shook, and I knew shock was setting in. "You can't help her now, so let it go."

"You don't know who I am. You don't know what I'm capable of." I yanked his shoes off and grabbed a toenail with the pliers. I held his foot down while I pulled up. Slowly.

Blood pooled from his toe, and he yelped and fought against the restraints. "Fuck! Stop!"

Beads of sweat crossed his forehead. His chest heaved as he worked to catch his breath. I yanked the last of the nail off and held it up. "One down, nine to go."

His eyes widened. "Okay! Stop. Let me talk!"

I dropped the nail and gripped another one. "You have two seconds to tell me who has Bryer."

"A man named Bandito."

That had my attention. I looked over at Callie, who had turned pale.

"Talk." I set his foot down and grabbed my gun.

"He came to me yesterday." Tears fell down his face. He licked his lips. "He told me he knew you had fallen for my daughter and that he had a debt to settle. Something about blowing up his island. He wanted to make a deal. He gave me a check. Said I just had to tell him where to find Bryer and look the other way."

"You fucking prick. You sold your stepdaughter, but you didn't know her monster was worse than the one who paid you." I pressed the gun to the back of his head. "Where is he? How do I get ahold of him?"

Rick shook his head frantically. "I don't know," he stuttered. "He came to me. He found me at the restaurant. The check wasn't even in his name. He used an alias."

Of course he did.

Fucking Bandito. What was he playing at? Why kidnap Bryer? She didn't blow up his resort.

Callie stepped closer and grabbed Rick by the balls. "What did he look like? Think hard."

He cried out and wriggled, trying to break free from her grasp. "He's gotta have a Spanish descent. Dark hair. A fucking mustache." He screamed as Callie twisted. "God, stop, please. I told you."

She didn't let up. "Not enough. You described half of Elko. Give us something more."

"Fine!" He cried openly now, sobbing.

She yanked her hand back and slapped him across the face. "Vaffanculo! You pissed on me!"

His pants were now soaked in blood and piss. I cringed. "That didn't take long."

She wiped her hands on his face. "Fucking gross."

Better her than me. I checked my watch. We'd been down there for almost an hour. To be fair, he lasted longer than I thought he would.

He was now gasping and choking on his own spit as he cried. "He's a cop."

A cop? Damn it. We would have to bring Rodriguez in on this and have him scour his entire force until we found this asshole. I squeezed the trigger.

"Damn it, Jax! Next time, wait until I'm not in the spray zone. Fucking asshole."

I grinned. "That's what you get for playing twenty million questions with Bryer in the truck."

She rolled her eyes and wiped her face. "I'm gonna need more than a shower. Do you know how hard it is to get blood out of clothes?"

"I have a feeling you've had some experience with that."

She lifted a shoulder. "So, do you think he was talking about a local cop?"

"Yeah. And it would make sense how he's been able to keep tabs on us so well. Like he's always two steps ahead of us." My jaw set.

Callie's shoulders slumped as she wiped her hands off on her pants. "I wish the guys were here."

I hung an arm over her shoulders. "I know. Me too."

"What do we do with him?" She gestured to Rick. His body hung limply off the seat.

"I'm gonna let him stay here until I can get a clean-up crew. I'll have to call one soon, but with everyone gone, we don't have time for that."

My phone rang, and I answered. "You are a hard man to get a hold of."

I didn't recognize the voice. "Who's been trying to get a hold of me?"

"I think you know who." There was a shuffle behind the phone. "I'm here with someone you might be interested in. Spicy little minx. When Bandito had me take her, I didn't understand your attraction for her, but now..." He grunted. "I'm seeing all the possibilities."

"If you fucking touch her—"

"I know, I know. You'll kill me. It's always the same response with you Cardosa men." He knew exactly who we were. "Would you like to say hello?" There was another shuffle.

"Jax!"

Bryer's scream shattered my heart. "Baby girl, listen to me. I'm coming for you. Don't stop fighting."

"Aw, isn't that sweet? You really think we'd let her live long enough if you got close?" He sounded so sure of himself.

I felt the world crash down around me. "What do you want?" I knew not to give in to their demands, but maybe I could keep him talking enough that I could hear something to help me pinpoint where he was.

"Bandito wants you all to die. Including your bitches. But I don't know, man. I might keep this one for myself."

"He's just trying to get under your skin," Callie whispered.

I knew that, but it didn't make it easier to hear. I clamped down on my toothpick. "How about we meet. Then you can kill me, and your boss can give you a raise."

"Now you're talking. How about you come find me at the quarry in thirty minutes. If you're late, I can see how long it takes to crush her pretty little head. I'm guessing not long."

"Which quarry? There are three of them around here." I was already thinking about where they were on the map.

"That's the fun part. I'm not telling you. The clock's ticking." He ended the call, and I gripped the phone so tightly a crack shot across the screen.

"Fuck."

Callie placed a hand on my shoulder. "We've been through worse. We'll find her. But right now, we gotta move. We have thirty minutes."

She raced up the stairs, and I followed her, taking two steps at a time.

Bryer's mom was sitting on the couch, alert but looking like she'd been fighting a bear. Lily was with her. She looked at me as soon as we emerged from the basement.

Sam rounded the corner. "I assume we need to move the mom and order a clean-up crew?"

"Yeah, but we have thirty minutes to find Bryer."

"Thirty minutes?" Fox stood at the door. It was the first time I'd realized he came with them. He looked like shit, and rightfully so. What happened with Bear's phone call was still raw and painful.

I nodded. "She's at a quarry, and I have thirty minutes to find her, or she dies."

Sam stepped further into the room. "I've got them. We'll get the mom to safety and then start looking for her. Which one are you starting at?"

I made it to the door and thought about it. "There's one by the dump, one outside of town toward the radio towers, and one by the mine parking lot. I'll start with the one in town and then head toward the radio towers."

"We'll go to the last one." Sam sprinted with me outside.

I ran to the truck and revved the engine. Jamming it into drive, I sped off. The speed limit didn't apply to me. Bryer's life was at stake. I checked my watch. I had twenty-four minutes left. Fuck!

I pulled into the first quarry and slammed on the brakes. A few workers milled around, but nothing made me think this was the one. I trusted my gut.

I slammed on the gas, spraying gravel and dirt everywhere. The truck fishtailed, but I kept going until I hit the dirt road past the businesses and older homes.

Hold on, little wolf, I'm coming. Don't stop fighting.

Chapter 21

Bryer

Fear clutched its cold fingers around my heart and squeezed. The guy who called Jax yanked Alice to stand.

She spit in his face. "Fuck you. Prick."

I raced over, jumping on the man's back, trying desperately to get him to let her go, but a second man came in and grabbed me, pulling me off of him. I kicked and thrashed as wildly as I could.

"Alice!" I attempted to ram the heel of my foot to the man's groin, but he dropped me on the floor.

Every bruise from my fall down the stairs screamed at the sudden impact. I groaned, moving away from him. Each inch I scooted toward the wall was like a mile.

"Shut the fuck up," he snarled at me.

The other man had already dragged Alice out of the room. Her cursing echoed in the hall, and another door slammed shut, muffling some of her beratement.

I tried to ignore her cries and the man's grunts. My life had been so desensitized to those noises, but I couldn't block them out this time. Not when it was my friend.

My stomach rolled. I wrapped my arms around my middle and rocked back and forth on the floor.

A few minutes later, she was pushed into the room. Her pants were around her ankles, and her hair was wild, like he'd used it to hold her down. The mascara smeared under her eyes was the only proof she'd cried.

Both men left, locking the door behind them.

Alice pulled her pants up and kicked the door. Screaming at him to let us go.

"Alice," I whispered.

She turned to me. Disgust and anger fueled her stare. "It's fine. I can't talk about it, or I'll break. I'll break later. After I kill him."

She returned to pounding on the door, trying the handle, and kicking it. "Your dick is smaller than a peanut!"

I pulled myself to sitting and rested my head back on the wall. We were in an office with nothing more than a barred window and a sealed vent. There was a desk and a chair, but nothing in the drawers. I knew because that was the first place I looked.

Alice tried to remove the vent to crawl out of the shaft while I searched for weapons. We both came up empty-handed. And so, we sat there, waiting for our end.

Jax said he was coming, and I knew he was, but I didn't think he'd make it in time before I was taken to the other room. Or worse... my head crushed like a grape. I heard our kidnapper tell Jax about that part. How much time did we have left? Ten... maybe fifteen minutes?

Pop. Pop. Pop.

Gunshots echoed throughout the building. I jumped, instantly alert. I wasn't ready to die.

Both kidnappers ran into the room, bolting the door behind them. Their guns were drawn, but neither looked confident in using them.

"Fucking Bandito owes us more than a hundred grand for grabbing this bitch!"

"Shit. I should have known Cardosa's men would come after us. There's a reason why the other pendejos wouldn't take the job."

My heart skipped a beat. Was it Jax outside that door?

I got to my feet and looked at Alice, who stared at me like I held all the answers. I mouthed, *Jax.*

She released a slow breath and inched toward me.

"Where the fuck do you think you're going?" The man who raped Alice stalked toward her. "You both are going to do everything I say so we can get out of here."

"I'd rather die than help you." Alice sneered and looked like she could throw up on him if he got closer. "Jax! We're in here! Help!"

The asshole raised his gun. "Wrong choice." He squeezed the trigger, and Alice fell.

Blood spatter sprayed me, and I screamed.

Darting over to her, I dropped to my knees. *Oh, God. Oh, God. Oh, God.* He had shot her in the head, and I knew there was nothing I could do to save her. She was already gone, but it didn't stop me from trying. I ripped a strip off my shirt and bunched it up, pressing it to the horrific wound.

"It's okay. You're gonna be okay." I squeezed my eyes shut.

Hot, sticky blood pooled around my knees, and I choked back the sobs as I pressed harder. "No. Please."

A gun pressed to my temple. "Get up."

I managed to rise on shaky legs. Alice's body lay lifeless at my feet. There was so much blood. I looked down at myself. I wasn't entirely sure it was all blood, and my stomach rolled.

Oh, God.

Someone pounded on the door, ramming it hard. "Bryer!" Jax yelled for me.

My kidnapper pressed the barrel harder to my head. "You say exactly what I say, or you'll end up like your friend. Tell him to let us leave."

I nodded. Tears streaked down my face. "Jax," I whimpered.

"Fuck. Angel, is that you? Come on out." The door handle hit the chair, and I heard him curse.

I cried harder. "There's someone in here with me." My breath caught in my throat. "You need to let them leave, or he's gonna kill me."

"Fuck!" Jax roared like the angry beast he was. "I swear I will kill every last one of you!"

"We have your girl. I don't think you're in the position to make threats."

"If she dies, I will draw out your death until you are begging to die, but I'm the fucking devil." Jax slammed into the door, and the frame cracked. It wouldn't be much longer, and he'd be in.

The gun was pressing so hard against my head that it hurt. I let out a small whimper, and Jax began ramming the door again.

Then, everything went silent. It was eerie how deadly quiet it was. "Jax?"

"I'm still here, angel. I'm coming for you. Don't you dare stop fighting." His footsteps sounded like they were running away from the door, and my heart sank.

"Fuck this shit. Harper!" The other man called out for Jax. "I'll make you a deal. I'll give you Bandito. Your girl. Fuck... anything you want."

A door slammed, and then more footsteps raced to the door. Jax laughed on the other side. "You're a special kind of stupid if you think I will let you live after touching my girl."

I know it was the wrong time, but my heart raced at hearing Jax call me his girl. If I was his, then I wasn't going to go down without a fight. I would be brave and strong. Like Alice was.

"Kill them all!" I yelled at him before twisting out of my captor's arms, catching him unaware and pushing him back.

He tripped over Alice and landed hard. His gun went off. The bullet ricocheted off the desk and embedded in the wall.

Jax broke through the door, barreling in with his gun drawn.

Bang.

Bang.

Two shots, and he lunged for me. Taking me into his arms, he held me tight. "Shh. I've got you. You're safe."

I was always safe with him. I was never leaving his side again.

"Alice," I murmured in his chest.

There was a slight pause before he spoke, "There's nothing we can do for her now, baby girl." He pulled me out and looked at me. "Are you hurt? Did they…"

He choked on the words.

I shook my head. "No. But they hurt her. They raped her. She was so brave, and they killed her." I wasn't sure if I'd ever stop crying. My poor friend.

Dani rushed into the room. "Bryer?" He looked down and saw Alice. The color drained from his face. "Fuck."

Callie came in behind him. "Damn, brother. You left a crumb trail of bodies." She noticed Alice and her face softened as she looked at me. "Are you okay?"

I didn't have a response. I wasn't sure what I was. "I'm alive."

"I get it. Ask me why I hate basements some time. When you're ready to talk." I had a feeling Callie had more trauma hiding behind the sarcastic façade she gave everyone. It was her way of coping.

"Let's get you out of here." Jax wrapped an arm around my shoulders and led me from the room.

I hated leaving Alice like that. Looking over my shoulder, it was hard to know that was it. She wasn't coming with us. She didn't make it.

"Don't look back, baby girl." Jax guided me from the house before taking out his cell. He dialed a number and waited. "I need you to come down to the old quarry outside of town and do your magic." He paused. "You have a bigger mess than you know. Don't bring anyone else from the force. You're gonna have to call in silent contractors." He continued giving what I assumed were clean-up orders to someone before ending the call.

He kissed the top of my head and walked me to the truck. The sun had already gone down, but it wasn't just the night air that had me shaking. I couldn't believe I'd been kidnapped and watched my friend die in a matter of hours.

Jax picked me up and placed me in the passenger seat but held onto me. He pulled me in, burying his face in the crook of my neck. "Don't give up on me."

I combed my fingers through his hair and held him to me. "Never."

His frame shook as he fought to regain his composure. I leaned my cheek on his head and let the tears fall. "I was so scared you wouldn't get here in time."

"I will always come for you."

I think he knew there was a chance he wouldn't have made it. Alice was proof that every second counted. My heart broke all over again.

Jax leaned away only to pull me to his chest. He rubbed my back and kissed my head. "You're safe now. I've got you. I'm not going to ever let anything else happen to you. I promise."

"You can't promise that." I hiccoughed.

"You let me worry about what I can or can't do. Have I ever lied to you?"

I shook my head.

He wiped the tears from my cheeks. "I promise you, Bryer. From this day forward, I will keep you safe. I will never let anyone take you from me again."

I believed him. His words were like blood, sealing a contract with a villain. I spent my whole life wishing for a knight but needed a monster. A beast. A vigilante to burn the world down and shoot the bad guys.

I pulled back and stared into the eyes of the man who killed for me. "I've decided I want to make it a rule you have to seal every promise with a kiss."

His mouth curved into a wicked grin. "Angel, I think your wings have fallen. Are you asking to kiss the devil?"

"I'm not asking." I leaned forward and pressed my lips to his. He was the only one who could ground me and make me feel as if I were floating at the same time. He stood between me and the demons.

The kiss broke too soon, and I sat there, letting him hold me. I looked around and realized I couldn't see anyone moving in the dark. I stiffened. What if there were more out there?

"Hey, look at me." Jax tipped my chin up. "Do you think I would put you in danger?"

I shook my head, but my heart raced irrationally so.

Two pairs of headlights lit up the old dirt road.

"Don't worry. It should be Sam, Lily, and Fox, and if he's smart, Rodriguez."

I tensed. "Who's that?"

Jax continued to rub small circles on my back. "He's a detective Jacob has on retainer."

A truck pulled up next to us, and Sam got out of the driver's seat. I couldn't believe they all came for me.

She scanned the area. "I assume everyone's dead."

"They took my girl. What do you think?" Jax held me possessively to his chest. His words vibrated into my soul, warming me in a cocoon of strength.

"What the fuck, Jax?" A man's voice barreled over the hood of the truck, and a mousy-haired, slender man strolled over to us. In the headlights, he looked like he aged ten years when he saw Jax's glare.

"You forget who you work for?" Jax was calm, but damn, the authoritative voice was something I couldn't ignore.

"I know who I fucking work for. But he's not here." The man looked around.

"Jacob writes the checks, but you work for all of us. Or do you need a reminder?" Jax didn't lose an ounce of his authority.

The man, who I assumed was Rodriguez, snorted. "You all are strung too tight. Would it hurt you to get laid once in a while? Fuck. You kill everyone, and don't think about how hard it is for me to clean it up."

"That's why we pay you. So we don't have to think about it." Jax gestured to the building. "There's a young lady in there. I was too late to save her. Make sure she is cared for."

Rodriguez furrowed his brow. "There were two girls? I thought there was only one."

Jax shifted so slightly that I was sure I was the only one to notice. "I never confirmed that with you."

Rodriguez hung his head and rubbed his neck. "Well, damn, I'm sorry. Was it... was it someone you were close with?"

Lily stepped around the truck, her hands on her hips. "Now I know my husband doesn't pay you to stand around and chit-chat."

Rodriguez's eyes widened. I bet he didn't expect to see her. "I thought you were gone."

"Plans change."

An ambulance pulled in, lights off. Strange. I thought sirens would be blaring and about ten more cop cars following suit. There was a massacre with gunshots. No way that was ignored.

Lily came over to us. "Go ahead, Jax. I've got her."

She took his place beside me as he walked off with Rodriguez and the paramedics.

"I don't like it. Something is off." She followed the men as they walked into the building. She gestured to Fox, who stood idly by, waiting for any orders.

I was sure everyone was still pissed at him, and he was probably stressed out. But at least he was here.

"Fox, go with them." Lily waited for Fox to leave and then had Sam and Callie come over. "Did you girls get that feeling?"

Sam shuddered. "Yeah. Something isn't right."

Callie looked over her shoulder. "If we all feel it, then whatever happened here tonight isn't over."

My stomach dropped. "You mean..."

Lily took my hand and gave it a pat. "There is never a dull moment in this family. If you can't do it... if you can't handle the intensity. Leave. Don't string Jax along because it will kill him."

I yanked my hand back. "I have no intentions of leaving. I have survived my entire life with *so-called* intensities."

Lily grinned, and Sam laughed. Callie bumped her hip with my leg. "She is a badass. I can see it. She's gonna make one hell of a sister."

Sam clicked her tongue. "I call dibs on teaching her to shoot."

Lily raised her brow. "You stick with the knives. I'll teach her to shoot."

Callie laughed. "You could always rock, paper, scissor it."

"Fine." Sam raised her hands up in rock position.

Lily rolled her eyes, lifting her hands. "I can't believe I'm doing this."

I almost forgot why we were there until the paramedics came out of the house with a stretcher. A single black body bag was strapped to it.

I hopped from the truck and ran over to them. "Wait!"

I reached for the zipper, but a hand stopped me. Jax pulled me back. "You were in shock when you saw her last. It's best if you don't see her."

In my head, everything about the moment she was shot was fuzzy. I couldn't remember what she looked like or what her gunshot wound did to her. I just remember pressing a piece of my shirt to her to stop the bleeding, but it didn't work.

I crumpled to the ground, but Jax caught me. Someone was crying, wailing into the night, but they were too far away. Too far from where I was to care.

Jax held me, pulling me to his lap. "Shhhh."

I sat cradled in his arms for what felt like hours. I sniffed and looked down at myself. With just headlights to give any light, I wasn't sure, but it looked like I was covered in blood.

"Oh, God. Get it off me." I began pulling my shirt off, needing it to stop touching my skin. Up and over my head, I chucked it as far as I could and sat there in my bra. That felt oddly cathartic.

Jax didn't say anything as he stripped his shirt from his torso and slipped it over me. I was instantly comforted by the warmth and scent that enveloped me.

"Hey," Jax cooed. "You're okay now."

I nodded. "I will be. I just need to get home and a hot shower." I wanted to scrub my skin until it was raw. I didn't want any remnant of this night left on me.

He scooped me up, standing, and carried me to the truck, putting me back into the passenger seat. He pulled out the jacket he loaned me the first night we met and wrapped it around me.

How lucky was I that I ran into this man and caught his eye. "Thank you." I wasn't sure if I could ever express my gratitude. Thank you seemed too cheap. Too lazy.

"Angel, you don't have to thank me for anything. This jacket? It's yours. These hands? Yours. My heart? Yours. I told you I was a devil and would do vile things for you."

"I still don't see a devil."

Ignoring me, he made sure I was settled in and told the others we were leaving.

I watched as the ambulance drove off. I wasn't sure why there was only one when more bodies needed to be removed. "How many were there?"

Jax climbed into the driver's seat and revved the engine, putting it in drive. "What?"

"How many did you have to kill?"

"There were only five." He said it so casually like this was literally another day on the job for him.

"You killed five men to save me?" It might not be a big deal to him, but to me, that was huge! Five people died by Jax's hand, all to get to me.

He grabbed my hand and pulled it to his mouth. He kissed my knuckles. "Baby girl, I would burn the world for you. There isn't a soul I wouldn't kill if they touched you."

Chapter 22

Jax

It was midnight before Bryer fell asleep. Exhaustion took over until she couldn't fight it anymore. Her soft snores against my chest made me grin.

She was safe.

I tightened my hold on her and kissed her head. My mind wouldn't shut off. I kept replaying the entire day over and over.

I still hadn't heard from Jacob, and each passing hour made my heart sink a little more. Without removing Bryer from my arms, I reached over and quietly opened the nightstand to grab a toothpick. There was so much about today that bothered me.

How did Bandito know where to send his men? How did they know she was in town? The girls were right. Nothing about today's events were finished. It was like a game to Bandito; he only moved a piece on the board.

I swear he was toying with us. Purposely trying to piss us off so we would stop thinking and act irrationally. And now I knew that it was someone close… possibly too close. Jacob would need to know what I learned with Rick, but right now, the focus must be on finding Bear. It was hard not to race back to Idaho and hike the mountain, but Jacob was right. We couldn't all do it, and keeping the queens of our family safe was just as important.

Bryer stirred, moving her leg slightly over mine. Fuck. An inch higher, she'd be stirring awake for a different reason. My little wolf. She was quickly becoming my everything.

I had always been a bit jealous of the others who found someone to fill that empty spot in their lives. Our line of work made us lonely creatures by choice... and necessity. Finding someone who could handle this life was rare.

But Bryer had been raised in it. Abuse is abuse. And there wasn't a day she hadn't survived it. While we tried to save those thrown into the pits of hell, she was born there, living the other side of our lives. She never condoned me or freaked out when I killed those men. She accepted me and what I do. It was a gift I wasn't going to refuse.

Putting the toothpick on the nightstand, I snuggled in closer to her. "I promise I will die before I let anyone hurt you again."

A soft snore was my only response. Closing my eyes, I attempted to fall into a fitful sleep.

The building got farther away with every minute that went by. I kept checking my watch, and I knew time was running out. Fuck! Bryer was going to die because I wasn't fast enough.

Checking my gun, I slammed the brakes and jumped out of the truck. I wasn't sure how I made it to the building, but I didn't care. There was a guard outside. I didn't hesitate to pull the trigger.

This had to be where she was. I entered the first floor, but the walls shifted to another building from a long time ago. What the fuck?

I jogged up the stairs, slitting a man's neck and shooting another one.

"Jax!"

I slammed into the door. "Bryer!"

The door flung open, and I saw a man with his pants down, fucking my girl. Rage burned through me like I'd never felt before. I shot him and then yanked him off her. But it wasn't Bryer. It was Alison.

She was scared and backed away. "Get away!"

I was so confused. Picking her up, I flung her over my shoulder and darted from the room.

A gunshot rang out, and I felt her body shudder. No! I lowered her to the floor, but Alice's face stared up at me.

"Jax!" Bryer cried for me.

Fuck. Where was she?

"I'm coming, angel!" I left Alice on the stairwell and began kicking in every door down the long corridor. Door after door had me looking into an empty room. A clock over each one ticked down to her death.

"Jax!"

"Fuck! Where are you? Baby girl, just tell me where you are."

For every door I went through, two more appeared.

A gunshot echoed through the building, and Bryer screamed.

Life ceased. No air to breathe. My heart froze.

"Jax!"

Someone gripped my shoulders and shook me. The hall disappeared, and I tensed.

"Jax."

Grabbing my gun, I sat up in bed and looked around.

Bryer was next to me, concern etched on her face. She touched my cheek. "And I thought I'd be the one to have nightmares."

Fuck. It wasn't real. I had found her in time.

I set the gun on the nightstand and wrapped her in my arms, holding her tight. We stayed like that until my breathing slowed down.

"Wanna talk about it?" She gripped my shirt and snuggled into my chest.

"I couldn't save you. The clock was ticking down, but you just kept getting farther away."

"But you did find me. You saved me."

But there were others. "You have every right to hate me. I couldn't save your friend."

"Jax Harper." She sat up and grabbed my face. "You will not save everyone. I learned a long time ago you have to save yourself. I wanted someone to rescue me, sure, but it was up to me to live. Surviving is more than a heartbeat. Alison couldn't live with what happened to her. That was her choice. And I don't think Alice would have been able to either. I think that's why she kept taunting the asshole."

His eyes gleamed with a sheen of tears. "It still hurts. I keep thinking that if I was stronger, faster, more alert, I could rectify their deaths."

"Jax, you might think you're a monster or some devil that decides when and how people die, but you're just the hand that pulls the trigger."

I scoffed. "Baby girl, you really are blind without glasses."

She slapped my chest. "Not funny." She playfully glowered at me. "I know what I see. And I love it all."

"Love huh?"

Even in the dark, I could see her blush. "There's room for growth."

I pulled her to me and kissed her. Her lips were soft and silky under mine. "I've decided I love you too."

"Just now?" She teased my bottom lip before trailing along my jaw to my throat. God, she was like fire, burning me alive.

I reached under her shirt and cupped her breast, eliciting a moan from her. "No. I decided that at the wedding."

The soft whimper she gave made my cock twitch. "Took you long enough."

I gripped her wrists and flung her onto her back. Bracing myself over her, I kissed under her ear and down along her collarbone. "Baby girl, I had to wait forty years for you. I wasn't about to waste time when I knew what I wanted. Falling for you was the easiest thing I'd ever done."

"I survived twenty-two years so you could save me." A small whimper escaped her lips as I lifted her shirt and took a nipple into my mouth.

"And I'll keep saving you. Every day for as long as you let me." I licked the soft nub until it hardened into a peek. Covering it with my mouth, I sucked on it.

"Except..." Her breathing was ragged as she arched her back. "Except I don't need saving."

"Explain, little wolf." I nibbled harder, loving the tiny sounds she made.

"I need a beast who will fight a pack of wolves for me while I save myself." She cried out and wrapped a leg around me, pulling me to her. "I want the bodyguard I met at the wedding."

My cock throbbed in my sweats, pressing against her perfect pussy. "That man hasn't stopped guarding you since you bumped into him. I vowed that no other man would catch you again."

"Jax," she whimpered.

I tugged on her nipple and then licked. "Mhm?"

"I'm falling hard."

"Fall, angel. Your devil will catch you." And I would spend eternity making sure she never loses her wings.

I lifted the shirt from her and discarded it on the floor. She lifted her hips, helping me remove her shorts. She was bare underneath, and I couldn't help but want to praise her for being so ready for me.

I could see the glistening silkiness drip from her with only the light of the moon pouring in through the windows. She was so wet. Sliding my finger through her slit, I pulled away and sucked the taste of her off.

My cock was so hard. Taking off my sweats, it stood erect and ready to dive into my pretty little angel.

I loved looking at her and spread her legs wider. "You are so fucking gorgeous."

I couldn't believe this fierce creature was mine.

I pressed the tip of my length to her entrance and paused. I wanted to draw this out to last forever. I wanted to make her scream my name until there was no air left in her lungs. I wanted to make her come until her body gave up her soul.

She raised her hips, looking for more. I thrust into her, burying my cock all the way. I groaned. She was so damn tight it was a miracle I fit at all. Her walls stretched and tightened around me, pulling me in.

Her cries escalated the rhythm between us. I pulled out to grab a pillow and placed it under her hips. Her breathing hitched as I reentered her, diving deep.

"Oh, fuck. Jax!" She arched and curled into me as I thrust deep. She clawed at my shoulders and then down to my ass.

"You take me so good." I kissed her, lingering to taste every part of her. "Such a good girl. My little wolf."

I wrapped my arms around her legs and spread her wider, plunging deeper. Her pussy tightened, gripping my cock as I thrust.

She writhed under me, and I wanted to see her come apart while she took control. What would she look like when she decided how deep to take me?

I growled, flipping us both over. Gripping her hips, I held her up so only the tip of my cock was in her. "Fuck me, baby girl. Show me what you like."

Bryer removed my hands and held them above my head, leaning over me. Her breasts teased me as her nipples grazed my heated skin.

Her eyes sparked as she slowly sank onto me. Groaning, I lifted my hips, wanting to bury myself all the way. Her legs widened, and she took more of me until I was fully seated in her.

She sat up and tipped her head back, arching as her hips undulated. Her hands roamed over her breasts, cresting the perky nipples. She was a goddess, and I was her throne. She lifted up and then came back down.

Grinding her clit on me, I knew she needed more than just my cock. I pressed my fingers to her, letting her ride my hand as well.

She moved faster, panting and whimpering as her body tightened. She clawed at my chest. "Jax. I'm so close."

I pressed my fingers around her clit and felt her spasm around my cock. Her hips rocked back and forth as she rode it out. "That's it, angel. Fuck me."

She collapsed forward, and I grabbed her hips, holding her while I thrust up into her. My balls tightened, and I released inside her.

I rolled her over and went down, sucking on her clit. She was so wet with a mixture of both of us.

"I want to taste." Her husky whisper had my cock twitching. Maybe I'd not heard her right?

"You want to taste what we taste like, baby girl?"

She nodded.

My heart hammered harder than it ever had before. Fuck, she was perfect for me.

I lapped up everything that dripped from her and rose up, hovering over her open mouth. I let our mixed cum pour from my tongue to hers.

She moaned, swallowing every last drop.

I was already hard again. Fuck. I was right. I would never be satiated when it came to Bryer.

Morning came, and there was still no phone call from Jacob. The afternoon passed, and the silence in the main house was deafening. When the sun set and no one's phone rang, our hopes were dashed.

It had been two nights since the plane went down. They should have found them by now. It didn't make sense. Unless...

No. I wouldn't fucking entertain the idea.

Bryer sat next to me, her legs over mine. She was texting Dani from her new phone. He took Alice's death harder than anyone. He was currently at a bar, drowning his sorrows, texting Bryer.

I'd be jealous if I were anyone else, but I knew Bryer loved me.

Loved.

I grinned and rubbed her calves, watching her roll her eyes at something he texted. "He's an idiot." Her mouth twitched to the side. "But he's taking Alice's death hard, so I can't blame him for being one."

Dani might not be the protector Bryer needed, but others could use his strength. He might not be the one to burn the world, but he sure as hell was there when it fell. He would be perfect for the expansion at Ana's Place. I wonder if Jacob would think the same thing and made it a plan to talk to him soon about offering Dani the full-time position down there. We needed someone else, and from what I understood, he wanted out of this area. Maybe being able to help others would help him with losing Alice the way they had.

She set the cell on the side table and turned to give me her entire focus. "It's gonna be okay. I can feel it."

I smirked. "Oh?"

"Yeah. All these years of predicting the future to stay safe have given me superpowers. I'm telling you. It's gonna be okay."

My hand inched higher on her leg. "Superpowers?"

She shrugged. "I can read a room faster than anyone."

I bet she could.

"Hey, you two. Stop making out on my couch!" Lily set a carafe of coffee on the long dining table behind us. "I figured none of us would sleep tonight and might need this, so I had Maria make us a fresh pot."

Sam checked her phone for the hundredth time. But it was Fox who held my attention. He went straight to the pot of coffee, filled a mug, and took a seat.

He hadn't said much in the past few days. Damn it.

I got up, leaving Bryer on the couch with Callie coming to sit with her.

While they had girl talk, it was time for Fox and me to have one of our own. Brother to brother.

I gripped his shoulder as I passed. "Follow me out."

As I expected, he didn't respond but got up, leaving his mug on the table.

Outside was cold. Snow was falling again, and it wouldn't be long before we were locked in for a season. We'd park a few trucks lower down and use snowmobiles to get in and out, but for the most part, winter was our downtime.

I walked to the barn, shaking off the snow once inside. Grabbing a bucket of oats, I began filling the troughs with the treat for the horses.

Fox came in, shaking his head, letting the snow fall. "I hate snow."

I made it to the end of the line when I noticed Fox still standing at the entrance. "You gonna help or not? Grab a bucket. Get that side."

We worked in silence for a time. I set the empty bucket down and climbed up on the railing of an empty stall. "When I met Bear, I was lost. Only the missions mattered. Saving lives and hoping I could clear my conscience."

"And did you?"

I chuckled. "Clear my conscience? No." Shaking my head, I gave the wood beam a good slap. "We should talk."

Fox hesitated before climbing up beside me.

"I know you're upset about what happened. It's hard to think that could have been Bear's last phone call. But my pain isn't with you. It's with the situation. The possibility that Bear might be gone is hard for me. One of the reasons why I volunteered to stay behind. Selfish, but I wouldn't be able to handle his death. Or yours. Or any of us." I pulled out a toothpick and let it roll across my tongue. "I can kill a man seven different ways, but when it's someone I'm close to..." I shook my head. "I think it was easier for me and everyone else to direct their anger to you rather than to deal with what might be."

"I'd take his place if I could." He exhaled slowly. "I can't stop thinking about it."

"And you won't. Not for a long time." I didn't want to be the bearer of bad news, but things like this changed a man. He wasn't about to forget anything any time soon.

He frowned and picked at a splinter poking up off the beam. "What do I do?"

"You're gonna get off this rail, go in the house, and protect the family. Right now, we have a house full of women who can gang up on us and know how to kill... Keep them distracted. Show them you are there for them and can handle whatever is thrown our way."

"And if Jacob calls?"

That was the wrong attitude. My gut twisted. "*When* Jacob calls, we will be whatever they need."

He nodded and jumped down. "Hey, Jax." He spoke with his back to me. "I haven't slept since that day. I close my eyes, and all I hear is the phone ringing."

He walked off, not wanting or needing a response. He was going to have to find ways to heal. We all did.

Back in the house, Bryer and Callie were becoming best friends in the living area. Fox and Lily were chatting at the table over coffee, and Sam was in the kitchen pestering Maria. No doubt probably trying to learn how to make her famous sweet bread.

Lupe sat on the barstool overlooking both rooms. "Ah, mijo." He beckoned me over. "It looks like you have found your missing piece." He picked up his coffee and gestured to Bryer before taking a sip.

I sat on the stool next to him. "You already have a woman."

"I can appreciate beauty, mijo. I'm married, not blind." He smirked over his cup. "Besides, Maria would skin me alive if I traded her for someone *younger*."

I choked on a laugh. "Holy hell, Lupe. You're gonna get us both killed."

He laughed and set his mug down.

Bryer looked over, catching my stare, and grinned. Damn I was a lucky man.

I nudged Lupe as I stood. "Have any advice on a long and happy life?"

"Hell, life is short, and you have to choose happiness. My advice? Make sure she never has a day that she wonders if you love her."

I thumped him on the shoulder. "And here I thought you were gonna have some aged wisdom." I ambled over toward Bryer and Callie. "Ladies. Mind if I steal my girl for just a moment?"

Bryer blushed and took my outstretched hand. "My knight in shining armor."

I pulled her close and whispered, "You are blind, beauty. For I am nothing more than a beast."

She leaned into me. "I was wrong. That's not my favorite fairytale."

"Oh? I've changed your mind about monsters?"

She swatted at my shoulder. "No. I've just decided that ours is my favorite."

Epilogue

Jax

The Next Day

It had been a hundred and fifty hours since I fell for Bryer. Ninety-six hours since Bear's plane went down. Ninety-one since I'd found out. Eighty-seven since I volunteered to stay behind. Sixty-eight hours since the last time I killed a man. And almost forty hours since I'd slept.

To say this week had been a whirlwind was an understatement. I touched Bryer's leg, gently lowering it to the couch as I stood. I needed more coffee. Okay, need was a bad way to put it. I probably had enough caffeine in me to kill a herd of elephants, but I couldn't sleep.

Bryer and the others took turns catnapping on the sofa or in the guest room, never far away, but Fox and I were vigilant.

My cell rang, and Jacob's name flashed across the screen. Bryer sat up, clearly not as asleep as I'd thought. Everyone stopped what they were doing and looked at me. Even Lupe and Maria stood hand in hand, waiting for the news.

I swiped the screen and held my breath.

"That was the worst game of rock, paper, scissors I've ever played."

Holy shit. It was Bear!

I gripped the chair in front of me at the dining table. "Damn, brother, you sound like shit."

"Let's see you survive a plane crash and three nights on a fucking frozen mountain and see how you sound."

I didn't care how cheesy I looked, grinning ear to ear. I looked up at everyone. "It's Bear. He's alive."

"I'm glad to hear from you, too." He laughed. "Put Lily on for Jacob. I'll see you soon, brother."

After days of silent worrying, the house was buzzing. I passed the phone to Lily so she could talk to Jacob. Sam's phone buzzed with Diesel, and then Callie's quickly followed with her husband.

Bryer came over and looped her arm with mine. "I told you everything would be okay. Superpower, remember?"

I kissed her head. "You did." My heart was lighter than it had been in years. "Does that superpower work on anything else?"

She touched her lips in playful thought. "Hmmm, it's telling me I've fallen in love with a beast."

"It should be telling you more than that."

She pushed her brows together. "What am I missing?"

I leaned in so only she could hear me. "It should be telling you to run, little wolf."

She looked around. Everyone was preoccupied with the great news and talking on the phone to even notice she was now flushed and breathing harder. "Jax."

"You have three seconds."

Three... Two...

She bolted out the door, and everyone turned their heads.

Callie stepped toward the open door. "Is she okay?"

Lily lowered the phone. "Did you do something to upset her?"

Sam stepped between me and my prey. "If you hurt her, I'm gonna roundhouse your ass until you're a fucking puddle of blood."

I held my hands up. "You all are like a pack of she-wolves and scary as hell. I promise, hurting her is the last thing I'm going to do."

Fox hitched a thumb over his shoulder where Bryer took off. "You want me to go after her?"

I smirked. "Not on your fucking life." I stalked out the door.

Thank you for stepping into the world of **Men of Cardosa Ranch**. These stories aren't always easy—they're dark, raw, and full of broken men who would burn the world down to save the women they love. But at their core, they're about **survival, redemption, and the kind of love that refuses to be tamed.**

🖤 A Quick Note on Escapism 🖤

This is fiction—an escape into a world where mercenary men deliver justice, love heals even the deepest wounds, and danger is met with unwavering devotion. These stories are not meant to reflect reality but to provide a safe space to explore intense themes in a way that always leads to a satisfying ending.

If this book kept you up at night, made your heart race, or had you gripping your Kindle, I'd love to hear what you thought. **Leaving a review—even just a few words—helps other readers find these stories and supports indie authors like me.**

🖤 Tell me what you loved by leaving a review here:
https://www.amazon.com/gp/product/B0CNGRKH72

Your support means everything, and I can't wait to share more of this world with you.

Until next time,

Gracin

Burnt Skies

Sneak Peek

I wasn't supposed to want her.
Hell, I wasn't even supposed to be here.

Babysitting Hailey should've been a simple job—keep her close, keep her safe, keep my distance.
But when our plane goes down in the snow-covered mountains of Idaho, **keeping my distance is no longer an option.**

Now it's just the two of us.
No backup. No rescue. **Nowhere to run.**

The cold is relentless. The nights are brutal.
But nothing is more dangerous than the heat between us.

She's supposed to be off-limits.
She's supposed to be just a job.

But in the silence of the wild, with nothing but my arms to keep her warm, **the lines start to blur.**

And by the time we're found?
It's too late.

Because Hailey isn't just under my protection anymore.

She's mine.

Bear and Hailey's story coming soon!

ABOUT THE AUTHOR

Gracin Sawyer pours her heart into every story, crafting dark, intense romances where broken men will burn the world down for the women they love. Writing has always been her passion, and while she's published multiple paranormal and fantasy romances under another name, stepping into this new world of dark romance felt like coming home.

If she had her way, she'd live on a cruise ship, sailing to every corner of the world—but for now, responsibilities keep her anchored on land. Thankfully, she's happily married to a man who'd follow her onto the open sea in a heartbeat.

After raising four kids, they now have one married and two still at home, life is a mix of adventure and transition, but the love for storytelling remains constant. When she's not writing, you'll find her dreaming up new stories, planning her next getaway, or lost in a book that's just as intense as the ones she loves to write.

!

Made in United States
Troutdale, OR
03/22/2025